"You're out of d
Neil Saxton said

And his tone was mocking. "At least where I'm concerned. I admire a woman with guts. She's so much more of a challenge, both in bed and out of it."

"Your personal views of my sex are of no interest to me whatsoever," Rue ground out from between clenched teeth.

"No, I can see that," he agreed and for some reason his cool, insolent glance over her body from the crown of her head to her bare unpolished toes made her want to hide herself. Stupidly, she had a vivid mental image of herself at eighteen—pretty and silly, her nails painted, her clothes the very best.

"I came to ask whether you'd like to have dinner with me," he said. Rue stared at him in shocked disbelief.

PENNY JORDAN was constantly in trouble in school because of her inability to stop daydreaming—especially during French lessons. In her teens she was an avid romance reader, although it didn't occur to her to try writing one herself until she was older. "My first half-dozen attempts ended up ingloriously," she remembers, "but I persevered, and one manuscript was finished." She plucked up the courage to send it to a publisher, convinced her book would be rejected. It wasn't, and the rest is history! Penny is married and lives in Cheshire.

Penny Jordan's striking mainstream novel, *Power Play*, quickly became a *New York Times* bestseller. She followed this success with *Silver*, a contemporary novel of ambition, passion, and intrigue.

Books by Penny Jordan

HARLEQUIN PRESENTS
1193—POTENTIAL DANGER
1201—WITHOUT TRUST
1216—LOVERS TOUCH
1243—VALENTINE'S NIGHT
1265—EQUAL OPPORTUNITIES
1282—BEYOND COMPARE
1297—FREE SPIRIT
1314—PAYMENT IN LOVE
1324—A REKINDLED PASSION
1339—TIME FOR TRUST

HARLEQUIN SIGNATURE EDITION
LOVE'S CHOICES
STRONGER THAN YEARNING

PENNY JORDAN

so close and no closer

Harlequin Books

TORONTO • NEW YORK • LONDON
AMSTERDAM • PARIS • SYDNEY • HAMBURG
STOCKHOLM • ATHENS • TOKYO • MILAN

Harlequin Presents first edition April 1991
ISBN 0-373-11353-6

Original hardcover edition published in 1989
by Mills & Boon Limited

SO CLOSE AND NO CLOSER

CHAPTER ONE

Rue knew she had a visitor long before the old-fashioned bell-pull clanged in the small front porch. Horatio had started rumbling deep in his throat the moment the car pulled up outside. It would probably be Jane Roselle coming to collect the delphiniums she had promised to have ready for her. If so, she was going to have to wait for half an hour, because she was early, and Rue hadn't quite finished tying up the bunches.

Five years ago, when she had first started growing and drying her own flowers and herbs, she had had no idea how quickly her small business would escalate, or the pleasure it would give her, but then, five years ago she had not thought it possible that life could hold pleasure for her ever again. She had been wrong, though. Perhaps her enjoyment was not the kind a young woman in her mid-twenties would normally expect, because it did not encompass any of the things that the rest of the world might consider necessary for happiness. There was no man in her life, for instance—no lover or husband to share her small pleasures and pains. She had no children, no family of any sort, barring Horatio. But she was content in her aloneness, preferring it, even welcoming it for its security.

The bell clanged again, more impatiently, and Horatio's growl deepened.

Rue deftly tied another bundle of the tall dried flowers and then hurried across the stone-flagged floor of the drying shed to wash her hands in the old-fashioned stone sink in the corner.

Her home, Vine Cottage, had once been part of a much larger estate. Vine Cottage itself had housed the estate gardener and, because of this, attached to it was a large assortment of outbuildings, including the comfortably sized drying shed with its old-fashioned heavy beams so ideal for hanging her flowers from. Next door to it was a small two-storey stable with a boarded loft and thick stone walls that kept dry in the wettest of weathers.

From the doorway in the upper storey, which had once been used, with the help of its small hoist, to store animal feed for the winter, it was possible to see as far as the big house itself and the hills beyond, as well as to look over her own ten-acre field, which was now, as they approached the end of summer, a glorious mass of rank upon rank of rich colour as her flowers bloomed.

She was just approaching the most critical period of her busy year. A dry late summer and early autumn meant that she could pick her flowers at their peak. Wet, windy weather destroyed the fragile blooms and could mean a whole season's work going to waste.

Horatio whined at the door as she walked towards it. He was a dog of large size and indeterminate breed. She had found him abandoned half a mile outside the village three winters ago and, having been unable to trace his owners, had adopted him, or rather he had adopted her, she admitted ruefully as he followed her into the house.

Vine Cottage, with its small stone-mullioned windows, seemed dark and cool after the hot sunshine outside. The original cottage had grown over the centuries and the house was now in fact a good size, although the many interconnecting rooms made it awkward to traverse in a hurry, Rue acknowledged.

The small front hallway was little more than a tiny passage with no natural daylight. So when Rue opened the front door she was momentarily blinded by the sunlight, and had to blink rapidly as her eyes adjusted to its brightness, before she realised that her visitor wasn't the customer she had been expecting, but a total stranger...a total *male* stranger.

Instinctively her fingers curled into Horatio's collar, finding comfort in the soft fur and reassuring solid muscle beneath it, and as though he felt her tension Horatio uttered a deep-throated growl of warning.

'Miss Livesey?'

He had a very deep voice, as one might expect for a man of his height and breadth, Rue acknowledged, at the same time as she acknowledged that he was obviously not a man who was used to being kept waiting, if that faint tinge of impatience, hardening his words to incisive irritation, was anything to go by.

As she nodded in acknowledgement, he stepped forward. 'If I could have a word with you?'

And, although he phrased the words as a question, Rue was left in no doubt that he fully intended them as a statement of intent. She was forced to step back into the narrow darkness of the hall.

The man had to duck his head to step under the lintel. All the cottage doorways were low; that did not bother her, as she was barely five foot four herself, but it would be bound to cause her visitor a good deal of irritation were he forced to inhabit Vine Cottage, as by her estimate he was a good two inches above six feet tall.

Rue thought momentarily of the doorways at the big house, spacious, elegant doorways many of them, designed by Robert Adam to go with the spacious, elegant rooms they opened into. It would surely be difficult to find two more different environments than Vine Cottage and Parnham Court, but Rue knew which she preferred.

It seemed that she had no option but to invite her unexpected visitor into the pretty sitting-room to the right of the front door. The front of Vine Cottage faced south, warm sunlight spilling from the mullioned windows into the comfortably furnished room. Rue had decorated this room herself, lovingly waxing the beams and then painting their ancient plaster infills with a special lime wash stained palest ochre, which gave the plaster a soft, warm glow.

She had learned a good deal in the five years she had lived in Vine Cottage, she acknowledged, glancing slightly ruefully at her clean but very short fingernails. Five years ago she would not even have known the importance of painting traditional plaster infills with lime wash instead of modern paint—and five years ago she would certainly never have dreamed of doing such work herself.

As her visitor followed her into the sunny room, Rue saw him glancing appraisingly at her few good antiques: the chest of drawers which she lovingly polished with wax polish; the two chairs she had re-upholstered herself; the small bureau.

While he was studying her home, Rue studied *him*, and now that she could see him properly she was tensely conscious of the air of vital masculinity that emanated from him.

Here was a man who was used to making his own rules in life... who was used to giving commands and having those commands obeyed. Here was a man who was used to the feminine sex paying full dues to his maleness, Rue suspected, even though there was nothing remotely sexual in the way his gaze flicked assessingly over her own slender body, registering the delicacy of her fine bone-structure and the fragility of her frame. Her blonde hair was pulled back off her face in a ponytail to make it easier for her to work, her skin free of make-up.

Six years ago she would never have dreamed of letting a man—any man—see her looking anything other than immaculately made-up and dressed. Odd to remember how much store she had once set by such things. These days... these days she saw very few men, and when she did she was always glad when she was free of their presence. They made her feel on edge, resurrected memories she would rather have suppressed... made her remember.

She realised that the man was looking expectantly at her and, for no reason that she could think of, she flushed vividly.

She saw the amusement darken the steel-grey of his eyes, and instantly her own flashed dark green with anger. So he found her amusing, did he? She didn't offer him a seat, but asked crisply, 'How can I help you, Mr...?'

'Saxton, Neil Saxton,' he supplied for her. 'I understood that my solicitor had been in touch with you.'

The moment he said his name, Rue remembered it. Of course, this man hadn't come here wanting to buy her dried flowers or herbs ... one look at the expensively tailored pale grey suit he was wearing should have told her that much. The letter had arrived over two weeks ago, and she had stuffed it to the back of her desk, meaning to reply to it but somehow or other never taking time in the busy days that had followed.

'You're the new owner of Parnham Court,' she said huskily, and, as though he found her statement of what he already knew to be both irritating and time-wasting, he said curtly, 'Yes. You've obviously received my letter.'

'You want to buy my land and this cottage?'

'Yes. I need somewhere for a housekeeper to live. There's room at the court, but I like my privacy. This place would be ideal for her. Your land, as you know, runs down one side of my drive. I'm prepared to offer you a good price.'

As she listened to him, Rue felt her anger growing. Did he really think he could simply walk into her home and bully her, with his masculinity and his wealth, into selling it to him? Five years ago she had virtually crawled into Vine Cottage like a wounded animal seeking sanctuary, and like an animal she had hibernated here all through one winter, barely aware of the damp and the draughts...the tiles missing from the roof, the lack of proper amenities...the state of disrepair the cottage had fallen into, having been unlived in for almost eight years. And then, with the spring, she had gradually started to reawaken to life itself. She had looked around her new surroundings and seen, in the sharp, strong sunlight of those early spring days, the dust and the dilapidation.

Having no money, she had had to do most of the work on the cottage herself. It had taken her two years to make it the comfortable home it was today. Two years of going to night school to learn a variety of crafts. Two years of working so hard that she practically fell asleep standing up at night. And now Vine Cottage wasn't just a house...it was a part of her.

She looked at Neil Saxton with angry eyes. How dared he simply walk in here and assume that, because he was a wealthy man, he had the right to expect that she would be willing to sell her home to him, just because he wanted it? She opened her mouth to tell him that no money on earth could purchase Vine Cottage, and then she acknowledged that part of the blame was hers. She ought to have written to her solicitor and informed him that under no circumstances did she wish to sell either the cottage or the land.

'I'm sorry,' she said formally, turning her back on him so that he wouldn't see her apology for the polite sham it was. 'Vine Cottage isn't for sale, and never will be.'

'I see.' Without looking at him, she could tell from the clipped tone of his voice that she had angered him. 'Well, Miss Livesey... I think I ought to warn you that I'm a man who never takes no for an answer. Everything has its price,' he told her cynically, and as she turned round to deny it Rue flinched beneath the look in his eyes.

It seemed to say 'even you', and her breath caught in her throat, locked there on a huge wave of pain and fear. Once his comment might have been all too pertinent ... but over the last five years she had truly learned the value of her own self-respect, her own pride, her own independence and, most of all, her own peace of mind, and these were things that were so important to her that they were worth more than the most fabulous of king's ransoms. And all of them were directly linked with Vine Cottage. It was her security blanket ... her base ... her own special private place; and too late she realised that in allowing this man to invade it she had allowed him to bring in with him values and emotions that made her tremble a little with fear.

Horatio felt it and growled again, his ears flattening to his head.

He had a good deal of Alsatian in him, and when he bared his teeth, as he was doing now, he could look extremely ferocious. Neil Saxton, though, seemed totally unafraid. He clicked his fingers to the dog and made a soft sound under his breath that changed Horatio's growl to a whine, and from that to a fawning adoration that made Rue stand and stare in disbelief.

Over Horatio's head, her eyes met Neil Saxton's cool grey ones in shocked anger.

Instantly the masculine hand that had been fondling the dog's soft head was removed, a frown drawing the dark eyebrows sharply together. He had thick, dark hair, well-groomed, and so clean that the sunlight bounced light back off it.

As he moved towards her, the air in the room seemed to stir lazily, warmed by the sun, and Rue just caught a hint of some tangy and very male cologne that made her think of the coolness of lavender mixed with the sharpness of her favourite herbs.

'There's no need to get worked up,' the cool, masculine voice told her almost mockingly. 'I came here to make you a genuine offer for your property, not steal it from you.'

He said it cynically, anger just beginning to darken his eyes as though he found the thought of her defensiveness both unnecessary and ridiculous.

His cool words penetrated Rue's anger. She focused on him and the blood came rushing into her face as she realised what a fool she was making of herself. But, as she looked at him and read the mockery in his eyes, her common sense was defeated by her anger. Gripping hold of Horatio's collar, she told him fiercely, 'I'll never sell this house...never! Now, please leave.'

She didn't accompany him to the front door, but stayed where she was until after she had seen him walk down the front path and out of the gate into the village street where his car was parked. An expensive, gleaming Daimler saloon with new number-plates on it, she recognised absently as he drove away.

Only when she was sure he had gone did she move, almost stumbling into the hallway and, once there, locking the heavy front door with both its old-fashioned key and the bolts she had had put on

when she'd moved in. It was disconcerting to discover that she was actually shaking.

The telephone rang, and she took a deep breath
that hurt her chest as she went to answer it.

It was Jane Roselle, apologising and asking if it
would be all right if she collected the flowers she
had ordered in the morning.

Assuring her that it would, Rue walked back, not
into the sitting-room, but into the room on the left
of the narrow hallway—the original rectangular
cottage kitchen, which now served as her study-
cum-sitting-room and which was comfortably furnished with two large old-fashioned armchairs, one
either side of the fireplace, and the big, old desk
which had once belonged to her grandfather and
which really was out of place in the humble cottage
sitting-room, but which she had not been able to
bring herself to part with. What had once been the
outbuildings to the original cottage had now been
converted into a pretty kitchen-dining-room. Upstairs the cottage had three good-sized bedrooms
and a pretty bathroom. She felt comfortable
here... far more comfortable than she had ever felt
at...

She dismissed the thought, shivering a little as
she went into the kitchen and started to make some
fresh coffee. How long would it be before Neil
Saxton discovered that...? Her hand shook and
cold water splashed down on to it as the jug jolted.

She had heard that Parnham Court had changed
hands. The last people to own it had rarely used it;
there had been talk locally of them converting it
into a country hotel, but that had evidently come
to nothing and now it had been sold again.

An unlucky house, so some of the locals believed. The story went that the house had originally been built on the site of an abbey, and that stone from the abbey had been used in the construction of the original Tudor house, now concealed somewhere behind the impressive Georgian additions made in the eighteenth century. It was said that the man who had originally built Parnham Court had also been responsible for the destruction of the abbey, and that, because of that, he and the house itself had been cursed. Rue shivered again, and at her feet Horatio whined. He followed her everywhere and even slept on the end of her bed if she let him, although he had a comfortable bed of his own on the floor just outside her bedroom door. His presence made her feel comfortable and safe. It protected her from her own aloneness, and from the memories that haunted her during her sleepless nights.

Neil Saxton had gone away, but how long would it be before he came back? Even without his saying so to her in as many words, she would have known he was not the kind of man to give up on something he wanted. And he wanted her home and her land.

She knew why, of course. Once, this cottage and its land had been part of the Parnham estate, and then it had been left to its then incumbent, the head gardener, for the duration of his lifetime, after which its ownership would return to the estate.

Parnham Court was two miles or so outside the small village of Parnham Magna. The drive to the house was long and straight, bordered on one side by an impressive row of lime trees; but on the other side, spoiling the symmetry of the driveway, was her land...her field, the border of which went right up to the edge of Parnham Court's drive.

Her hawthorn hedge now grew where the lime trees must have once been, and her cottage disrupted the long, elegant line of the high brick wall which surrounded Parnham Court. Oh, yes, she knew quite well why Neil Saxton wanted her home. He wanted it so that he could destroy it.

He wasn't the first person to approach her with a view to buying her home. Only last summer there had been a builder, a tough, self-made man from a nearby city who had driven through the village and seen at once the possibilities of her home and its land with its valuable main-road frontage, in a small, rural area that would be so conveniently close to the city once the new motorway system was completed.

He had been very angry when Rue had turned his offer down.

It was a pity it was Saturday, otherwise she could have got in touch with her solicitor and asked him to write to Neil Saxton, making it plain that she had no intention of selling. If she hadn't been so busy she would have done so before now. But it had been a good summer for her. Her field was now crammed full of the flowers she grew to pick and dry. Only this spring she had planted up the last quarter of it, paying half a dozen teenagers from the village to help her with the work. Upstairs in the loft above the stable, she had rack upon rack of those spring and early summer flowers which had already been harvested.

She had never envisaged herself as a business-woman, but that was what she had become, albeit in a small way. Her talent for drying and arranging flowers had been something she had done merely for her own pleasure, until a friend had asked her if she would supply her with some of her arrangements, and her skill had spread by word of mouth until another friend had suggested she turn her talent into a full-time business.

It had helped having the new country hotel and club open less than ten miles away. The two young chefs who ran it had come to the house to buy dried flower arrangements for the hotel and, seeing the walled herb garden to the rear of the property, had begged her to sell them some fresh herbs. That side of her business too had escalated, and she now supplied not just them but several other local restaurants as well.

All in all, she had carved out a very pleasant life for herself, even if her friends did bemoan the fact that there was no man in it.

They all knew about the past, of course; it was impossible to keep a secret in such a small village, even if she wanted to, and they all respected her refusal to talk about what had happened. She suspected that the more romantically inclined of them thought her reticence was due to grief.

Grief... If only they knew.

Rue had to make the most of the long summer evenings, and it was gone ten o'clock before she tiredly acknowledged that she had had enough.

Calling Horatio, she set out in the direction of her field, opening the door in the wall that led to it.

Horatio knew better than to do anything other than stick to the narrow paths between the flowers. When his mistress paused to examine some blooms more closely or to test the richness of their scent, he too waited, knowing that, once her inspection was done, he would be allowed to run free along the footpath that ran behind her field and back to the village.

This was one of her favourite parts of the day, Rue acknowledged, savouring the colour of the tall spikes of delphiniums glowing richly against the evening sky.

Her other favourite time of day was early in the morning, just after dawn, when the dew was still on the grass and she felt as though she had the whole world to herself. She liked it that way: clean . . . new . . . uninhabited by anyone bar herself and Horatio.

As she finished her inspection and climbed the stile that led to the footpath, she saw in the distance the outline of Parnham Court. Lights shone at the windows; evidence, if she needed it, that the new owner was in occupation.

What was he doing? Reading in the quiet solitude of the panelled library . . . eating in the awesomely elegant crimson dining-room, or perhaps relaxing in the comfort of the south drawing-room?

Her own curiosity made her feel uneasy. She had never speculated about the inhabitants of Parnham Court before . . . perhaps because they had not come knocking on her door, spoiling her peace, making demands on her which she could not and would not meet.

Healthily tired, she made her way back to her cottage. Horatio, used to his mistress's evening routine, padded into the kitchen, waiting for her to make the hot milky drink she always took to bed with her.

CHAPTER TWO

AT TEN past nine on Monday morning Rue had just returned from checking her field—something she did meticulously twice a day during the height of the summer and early in the autumn, those all-important times of the year for her when even a couple of days' neglect could mean the difference between picking her flowers at their very best or finding she had left things too late and the petals were already beginning to shed—when the telephone rang. She picked up the receiver in one hand while she poured herself a cup of coffee with the other.

The unexpected sound of her solicitor's voice, faintly hesitant and apologetic, surprised her.

'I wonder if you could come in and see me,' he asked her. 'There are one or two things I need to talk over with you.'

Instantly suspicious, Rue told him, 'If it's about Neil Saxton's offer to buy the cottage and my land, then I might as well tell you that I'm not interested.'

'It isn't something we can discuss over the telephone,' her solicitor told her and, sensing his determination and knowing how much he had her interests at heart, Rue gave in and agreed reluctantly that she would drive in to the local market town and see him. He suggested taking her out for lunch, but Rue turned his invitation down, explaining to him that she was far too busy to be able to spare him more than half an hour of her time. She didn't add that she wouldn't have been able to spare him as much as that if she hadn't needed to go into her local market town to stock up on supplies. The village, lovely though it was, only had one very small general store, and Rue normally made the trip once a month to the local market town to stock up on groceries.

At eleven o'clock she bundled Horatio into the ancient estate car she had bought three years ago when her business had first started to grow. The car was old but reliable, its roomy rear-section ideal for carrying her stock.

It took her just over half an hour to drive into town. She parked her car in the pretty market square, empty on a Monday of the bustle of traffic which filled it to capacity on Wednesdays and Saturdays—market days.

Her solicitor's office was up a rickety flight of stairs in a tiny Elizabethan building, part of what had once originally been the old Shambles. Now the whole street was a conservation area, the shop beneath the offices a prestigious book store.

It was still possible, from the attic room at the top of the house, to reach out from the window and shake hands with somebody doing the same thing in the house on the opposite side of the street, but it wasn't the building's history which was on Rue's mind as she rapped on the outer door of her solicitor's office and walked into the small reception area.

David Winten had originally been her father's solicitor, and the two men would have been about the same age if her father had been alive. As always when she was invited into the tiny, cramped office, Rue was reminded unbearably of her father. He had married fairly late in life, and she had been born eighteen months after her parents married.

Tragically, her mother had died within hours of her own birth, and because of that, she and her father had shared a closeness which even now, six years after his death, she still missed.

'Rue.' Her solicitor's face creased in a delighted smile as he swept some papers off the chair and dusted it down apologetically before offering it to her. 'My dear, how lovely it is to see you.'

Rue hid a tiny smile as she accepted the chair. How on earth he managed to make a living out of his practice she had no idea. Every surface in the small room was piled high with pink-tied bundles of legal papers, files gaped open in half-open drawers, and a tortoiseshell cat drowsed in the sun coming through the small window.

'Neil Saxton came here to see me first thing this morning,' he told her rather breathlessly as Rue sat down. 'In fact, he was here waiting for me at half-past eight when I arrived.'

Immediately he mentioned Neil Saxton's name, Rue's face hardened. 'It's no good,' she told him firmly. 'Nothing you can say to me will make me change my mind. I'm not going to sell Vine Cottage or the land.'

'My dear child, think,' her solicitor pleaded with her. 'I assure you he's prepared to be very generous—very generous indeed. With that money...'

'I have more than enough money for my needs,' Rue cut in ruthlessly. 'I own the cottage and the land and its freehold. I have no debts.'

'And no assets, either,' her solicitor pointed out firmly, surprising her a little. 'Rue, think: at the moment your business is doing very well, but you have precious little behind you. A bad season, any other kind of accident...'

'You don't need to tell me that,' Rue interrupted him. 'But it isn't going to happen.'

'My dear, I can understand your attachment to the cottage and to the village, but surely there must be other properties.'

'I'm sure there are,' Rue agreed obediently, 'but I suggest you try telling that to Neil Saxton, and not to me.'

'But you must realise why he wants *your* property.'

'Of course,' Rue agreed.

'It was, after all, originally part of the estate,' her solicitor pointed out. 'He has told me that he is concerned that, if for any reason anything were to happen to you, the land could be sold away completely, and that is the reason he is prepared to make such a very generous offer.'

Rue's eyebrows climbed a little as she listened to this rather hesitant statement, hardly surprising, she reflected inwardly, in view of her comparative youth.

'You may reassure Mr Saxton that I have no intentions of selling the land either to him or to anyone else,' she said firmly, standing up. 'I'm sorry. I know you're only thinking of my future and my security, but Vine Cottage *is* my future and my security. I refused to sell it to that builder last year and now I'm refusing to sell it to Neil Saxton.

I'm sorry if he finds that knowledge unpalatable, but he'll just have to accept it.'

She saw that her solicitor was looking very unhappy, and hesitated, frowning a little.

'He's a very determined man,' her solicitor offered nervously. 'He asked me a lot of questions about you...about the land...'

Rue's frown deepened. 'What did you tell him?' she questioned sharply.

Her solicitor looked even more unhappy, and a tiny sigh of irritation escaped Rue's soft mouth. She should have known that a man like her solicitor would be no match for the Neil Saxtons of this world. By now, no doubt, he knew the whole sordid story of her past and the folly she had committed. She shrugged inwardly. What did it matter? He would think her a fool, of course, but what did his opinion matter to her?

'Well, if he gets in touch with you again, please tell him that there is absolutely no question of my selling the land either to him or to anyone else,' Rue said firmly.

'I don't think he's going to give up easily,' her solicitor told her warningly, 'not a man like that, who's built up a multi-million international company almost out of nothing.'

Rue hesitated, her interest caught in spite of herself. 'What exactly does he do?' she questioned her solicitor thoughtfully.

'His company deals in computer software of a highly specialised sort.' Her solicitor made a vague movement with his hands. 'I believe it's very high-powered, and that he himself has made a personal fortune from his own innovative ideas.'

'A self-made millionaire,' Rue mocked a little bitterly, 'and now that he's made it he's decided to buy himself a part of England's heritage in the shape of Parnham Court.'

As though he knew the pain that underlay her cynical words, her solicitor looked sympathetically at her.

'I'm sorry, my dear,' he said softly. 'I know how it must hurt you.'

Rue brushed aside his words impatiently.

'No, no, it doesn't at all,' she told him fiercely. 'I'm not so much of a dog in the manger.'

Her solicitor looked at her and waited, and Rue knew he was waiting for her to explain her antipathy towards Neil Saxton. Unfortunately, it was something she just couldn't do. She couldn't analyse even to herself the true reasons underlying her instinctive dislike of the man. One thing she did know, though, was that, no matter what her financial circumstances might be, she would never sell Vine Cottage or its land to him.

And yet, when she stepped outside into the shadowed coolness of the narrowed street, it wasn't with a feeling of confident assertiveness because she had made it plain to her solicitor that she had no wish to enter any kind of negotiation for the sale of her property, but rather with a feeling of deep and unwanted unease. The kind of unease that prickled under her skin and made her muscles tense, almost as though she half expected Neil Saxton to appear out of nowhere and demand that she sell her land to him.

Horatio was waiting patiently in the car for her when she got back with her shopping. She stowed it away economically and then got into the driver's seat. She had wasted far too much time over Neil Saxton already, she told herself grimly as she drove towards home.

Once there, she removed her shopping from the car and packed it away, and then went upstairs to change into her working uniform of cotton T-shirt and jeans. The neat skirt and top she had donned for her visit to her solicitor were clothes that belonged more properly to the period before her father's death. She rarely wore such formal things these days, and indeed, had only put them on in the first place because she knew that her solicitor, old-fashioned perhaps about such things, would not have felt comfortable at the sight of one of his female clients clad in a pair of disreputable old jeans and a shabby T-shirt. Nevertheless, these were the clothes she now felt most at home in, she told herself, pulling the T-shirt on over her head and disturbing the smooth sleekness of her blonde hair as she did so.

She just had time to snatch a quick salad lunch before going outside into the field with her secateurs and her trug, ready to start harvesting those flowers that were at their peak. It was hard, back-breaking work, especially with the heat of the sun beating down on the back of her neck and her upper arms.

At three o'clock in the afternoon, as she straightened up tiredly, she acknowledged that she ought to have worn a hat. Her head was already beginning to ache, the pain pounding in her temples as she raised a grubby hand to massage the too-tight skin. Horatio had long ago deserted her to go and lie down in the shelter of the hedge. She thought longingly of her cool kitchen and the lemonade in the fridge there.

She was just on the point of giving in and going back to the house to get some when an all too familiar male voice hailed her. Furiously she watched as Neil Saxton climbed over the stile that separated his land from hers and came towards her, carefully weaving his way among the tall spires of her flowers.

Unlike her, he looked immaculate and cool. He was wearing a pair of white cotton trousers and a thin white cotton shirt open at the throat. His skin, like hers, was tanned, but his tan was much darker, richer. As he came towards her she felt a tiny pulse of fear beat frantically deep inside her body, and she had a compulsive urge to throw down her trug and take to her heels.

Telling herself that she was being idiotic, she remained where she was, unaware of how revealing the tight, defensive look on her face was to the man approaching her. He had learned a good deal from her solicitor this morning, and as he drew level with her Rue saw that knowledge in his eyes.

Mentally cursing her solicitor for his naïveté, she said coldly, 'If you've come to try to persuade me to sell my land, you're wasting my time.'

Instead of responding to her challenge, he turned away from her and gestured over to where the neat beds of herbs nestled in the shelter of her walled garden.

'Who buys those from you?' he asked her thoughtfully.

Surprised into giving him a response, Rue told him, 'Restaurants, sometimes gardeners wanting plants of their own, health food shops, and even people wanting to buy them for medicinal purposes.'

'You're joking.' His amused cynicism irritated her.

'No, I'm not joking at all,' she told him sharply. 'After all, herbal medicine existed long before our so-called modern drugs.'

'Well, yes, but they were hardly as powerful.'

His self-assurance annoyed her, and she had a sudden longing to destroy it.

'Some of them are,' she argued firmly. 'Take ergot, for instance...'

'Ergot... What's that?' She had his attention now, he was looking at her in a direct, uncompromising way that she knew that she ought to find intimidating, but which instead for some odd reason she found challenging.

'Ergot is the fungus on the rye,' she told him knowledgeably. 'It used to be used, among other things, for aborting unwanted foetuses. Unfortunately, its side-effects can be devastating. Used unwisely, it can give rise to a whole range of things from gangrene to madness.' She saw the look on his face and laughed harshly. 'It's still used today as a base for migraine drugs. Doctors prefer only to prescribe it for men,' she added drily.

'You obviously know a lot about it.'

Without thinking, she shrugged and said, 'It was my father's hobby. I grew up with it, so to speak.'

'Yes,' he agreed grandly. 'I think I can see why a man who's fortune was founded on modern drugs could be interested in herbal medicine.'

Instantly Rue tensed. He had tricked her—and she had let him, fool that she was, carried away by her enthusiasm for one of her favourite subjects—into betraying herself and giving him exactly the kind of lever he wanted to pry into her most private affairs. He wouldn't hesitate to use it, she could see that in his eyes as he looked at her.

'Your solicitor was telling me this morning about your father,' he added, still watching her. 'What happened?' he demanded abruptly when she refused to either look away or make any comment.

The abruptness of his question caught her off guard. 'To what?' she asked him uncertainly, not sure of the meaning behind his question.

'To the fortune your father left you?' he answered harshly. 'He died six years ago, apparently a millionaire, and yet you, his only child, are now living here in this cottage, instead of Parnham Court which he left to you, and apparently earning your own living—a rather curious state of affairs, I'm sure you'll agree.'

'To you, perhaps,' Rue answered him in a suffocated voice, almost totally unable to believe that she had heard him correctly. His rudeness was really insufferable. She opened her mouth to tell him as much and then, to her own shock, heard herself saying instead, 'If you really must know, my husband gambled it away and I let him.'

She faced him proudly, waiting to see the pity and contempt form in his eyes. But, whatever feelings her words had evoked inside him, he betrayed nothing of them as he said coolly, 'You must hate him for that.'

'No, not really. Odd though you might find it to believe, I'm far happier now than I ever was when I was my father's heiress. I was a spoiled, arrogant child. You could even say that I deserved everything that happened to me. There's no way today, for instance, that I would ever be remotely attracted to a man like Julian, and certainly I'd never be stupid enough now to believe him capable of loving me.'

'Him, or any man?' Neil Saxton asked her quietly.

The shock of it was reflected in her expression as her eyes darkened and widened. How had he known that? How had he known of the iron that had entered her heart when she'd found out the truth about Julian? How had he known that she had sworn that never again would she allow any man to deceive her into believing he cared about her?

She fought to regain her self-control, shrugging her shoulders and saying as coolly as she could, 'It's true. I'm afraid I don't have a very high opinion of your sex.'

'Or of yourself,' Neil Saxton told her, softly and unforgivably.

She turned her back on him then, gripping hold of her trug tightly in order to stop her hand from trembling.

'You're on my land, Mr Saxton,' she told him emotionlessly, 'and I would be very grateful if you would remove yourself from it immediately.'

'You know, you interest me,' he told her conversationally, totally ignoring her command. 'It must have taken guts to establish all this——' he waved his hand over the flowing river of colour surrounding them '—out of nothing. To turn yourself from a dependent child into an independent business-woman.'

Rue smiled mirthlessly at him. 'And men don't like women with guts, especially successful women with guts—is that what you're trying to tell me?'

To her astonishment he laughed, throwing back his head to reveal the hard, masculine line of his throat. 'Is that what you think?' he marvelled, looking at her. 'Is that the reason for this?' He reached out and touched her tightly drawn back hair and then her make-up-less face. It was only the briefest of touches, no more than a mere brushing of hard muscles against the softness of her smooth skin, but it was still enough to make her jump back from him as though she had been burned, rage and panic warring for supremacy in her eyes.

'You're out of date,' he told her mockingly. 'At least where I'm concerned. I admire a woman with guts. She's so much more of a challenge, both in bed and out of it.'

'Your personal views of my sex are of no interest to me whatsoever,' Rue ground out at him from between clenched teeth when she had recovered from the shock of his unashamedly taunting comments.

'No, I can see that,' he agreed, and for some reason the cool, insolent way his glance roved over her body, from the crown of her head right down to her bare toes with their unvarnished nails, made her want to turn and run and hide herself away from him. Stupidly, she had a vivid mental image of herself as she had been at eighteen, pretty and silly, her blonde hair a flowing mane, her nails long and painted, her clothes the very best that Knightsbridge could provide and her head empty of a single thought that did not concern having fun and enjoying herself.

It was too easy to blame her father for her hedonistic naïveté. He had loved her and indulged her shamelessly, but he had been too old to understand the pitfalls lurking to snare such a very young and unworldly girl as she had been.

She had had very few friends of her own age, and no female relatives at all. No relatives of any kind in fact, apart from her father. She had been taught privately at home and, although her father had taken her all over the world with him and had showered her with jewellery and pretty clothes, she had had no real experience of life at all. His death when she was nineteen had come as a tremendous shock, even though it seemed that the doctors had been warning him for years that he was overdoing things.

She was his only child and sole heiress and, more scientist than businessman, he had never thought to tie up her inheritance in a way that would ultimately protect her so that when Julian . . .

'I came over to ask whether you'd like to have dinner with me.'

The invitation shocked her out of her thoughts. She stared at him in disbelief.

'Dinner? With you?' Her mouth compressed. She was no longer an idealistic nineteen-year-old. She knew very well now that, when men paid pretty compliments and spoke falsely of love, their words were simply being used to mask other desires and other needs. Men were predators on her sex, using women to further their own aims and their own ambitions. 'Dinner? Are you crazy?' she questioned him sharply. 'I've already told you you're wasting your time. I have no intention of selling my home.'

'Oh, it wasn't as a possible purchaser of your land that I wanted to give you dinner,' he told her, enjoying the confusion which suddenly darkened her eyes before suspicion drove it away. 'No, it's your expertise in the art of floral décor I'm interested in at the moment. Don't think I've given up on getting your land, though,' he warned her. 'I can be very determined when I want something.'

'I'm sure,' Rue told him drily.

He laughed, apparently completely unabashed by the cool tone of her voice.

'My mother is coming to stay with me in a few weeks' time. I bought the house as it stands, but some of the rooms look a little bit dreary. I thought some dried flowers might add a slightly more welcoming touch, and I wanted to seek your professional advice and expertise.'

Rue looked at him, not sure of whether to believe him or not.

'Of course,' he added carelessly, 'I quite understand if you prefer not to come up to the house. I can see that visiting it might prove too painful.'

His suggestion that she might be jealous, that she might for one moment resent the fact he was living in her old home, goaded Rue into immediate retaliation.

'Not at all,' she told him swiftly. 'I don't think I have anything on tonight. If you'd tell me what time you'd like me to call—but there would be really no need for you to provide me with dinner.'

'It will be my pleasure,' he interrupted smoothly. 'I much prefer to cook for someone else other than myself. It's so much more rewarding, don't you agree?'

And, before Rue could hide her astonishment that such a very masculine man should actually admit to being able to cook, he turned and looked at her, his grey eyes alight with amusement. 'In fact, I wouldn't mind some cuttings from your herbs, once I've got the kitchen garden re-established. It's in a very run-down state at the moment.'

'Yes,' Rue remarked absently. 'The previous owners only visited the house on very rare occasions, and it's been badly neglected.'

She was curious to know why an apparently single man should choose to buy himself such a large house, and on an impulse she couldn't quite analyse she asked quickly, 'Do you live alone, or...?'

'Am I married or otherwise attached?' he supplied drily, making her flush with embarrassment and irritation. 'Neither. Just as for many another successful businessman, there never seems to have been time to establish any deep-rooted relationships, which is why I now find myself in my mid-thirties and somewhat isolated from the rest of my peer group. Everywhere I look these days I seem to see happily married men with wives and families.'

'A wife and family shouldn't be too difficult for a man of your wealth to find,' Rue told him cynically.

'That depends,' he responded and, without waiting for her to question him, he added, 'on how high one's standards are. Mine are very high,' he told her evenly, which meant, Rue reflected bitterly, that if and when he married it would be to some pretty and possibly well-born young woman whose looks would be a perfect foil for his success.

'I'll pick you up at eight o'clock,' he announced. 'We can eat about half-past eight and over dinner we can talk about the kind of floral arrangements you might be able to provide that would add a slightly softening effect to the house's austerity.'

'There's no need for you to pick me up,' Rue told him sharply. 'Heavens, it's only half a mile or so to walk, and besides, I do have transport.'

'I'll pick you up,' Neil reiterated in a voice that warned her that he was not prepared to listen to any further argument.

After he had gone, Rue stood where she was in the middle of the field, in a daze, wondering why on earth she had been mad enough to allow him to talk her into having dinner with him. The last thing that she wanted was to spend time in his company.

She didn't like him. Since Julian's death and the end of her marriage, she had kept her distance from all men, but most especially from those men like Neil Saxton, from whom emanated an almost tangible aura of male sexuality. She no longer deceived herself. The pretty, girlish bloom she had once had was long gone. She was not beautiful in the accepted sense of the word, nor did she want to be.

She had no desire at all to excite male admiration, and she was certainly not so stupid as to im-

agine Neil Saxton wanted her company because he
found her attractive as a woman. Once, long ago,
she had been foolish enough to believe that a man
loved her. She had paid a very heavy price for that
folly, and it was a mistake she was never going to
repeat.

As she bent over her work she told herself that
it was stupid to waste time thinking about Neil
Saxton. If there was any way she could have got
out of their dinner date she would have done so,
but she had to acknowledge that he was perfectly
capable of coming into the cottage and dragging
her out by force if he felt it necessary.

No, she would have dinner with him tonight, and
afterwards she would make it plain to him that she
wanted no further contact whatsoever with him.

At five o'clock, her back feeling as though it was
about to break in two, she made her last journey
towards the drying shed to empty her trug. The long
worktop under the window was inches deep in the
flowers she had picked that afternoon.

She had several hours' work ahead of her now,
preparing the flowers for drying. Over the years,
mostly by trial and error, she had evolved several
different methods of drying flowers according to
their various needs. Some of them could quite easily
be dried in bunches suspended from the ceiling
beams, others needed more delicate handling, and
these she spread in very fine nets which she suspended between the beams. Others still needed
drying in the warmth and darkness of the heated
room, and for that purpose she used the lower part
of the old stable, closing the heavy shutters on the
window to keep out the daylight. Some of the

flowers she left in their natural state, others she dyed in the more vivid shades that were becoming popular, especially among her more sophisticated clients.

Really, this evening she should have been devoting every minute of her time to her work. Angry with herself for wasting precious hours with a man whom she already knew she ought to be doing everything in her power to avoid, Rue made her way back to the house.

It was almost the end of the financial quarter. Soon it would be time to go through her books and prepare the returns for the accountant and the VAT officials. Her bookwork was the bane of her existence. She dreaded the two or three days a quarter she had to spend cooped up at her desk, checking and rechecking the tiny columns of figures she kept meticulously.

As she poured herself some lemonade, her mind shied away from the reality of her almost paranoic dread of this quarterly ordeal. It had nothing really to do with her ability to cope with the long columns of figures, and in fact sprang from the past. Julian had worked for her father's accountants. He had come to see her two months after her father's death. He had been so sympathetic and charming, so ready to spend time with her and listen to her, and she, lonely and bereft in those early months after her father's death, had been only too eager to have someone to lean on.

He had been ten years older than her, sophisticated and mature, and he had known exactly how to flatter and coax her, so that by the time he actually proposed to her she was half wild with love for him, or rather she had believed that she was.

It had taken just one disastrous night of marriage to show her the real Julian, the man behind the mask he had worn to woo her, the man who cared nothing for her at all and had only wanted her father's fortune. As always when her memories of the past threatened to spill over into the present, she fought to subdue them, to push them away, and she was glad when the telephone rang, giving her an excuse for doing so now.

It was one of the large city shops she supplied, asking if she could let them have some extra stock. It didn't take her long to run through her stockbook. Luckily she had plenty of what they wanted already dried.

Because she was so busy, she informed them that they would have to send someone out to collect their order, and by the time she had replaced the receiver she had got the past firmly back where it belonged—out of her mind.

CHAPTER THREE

RUE worked until seven o'clock, grimly refusing to allow herself her normal break as a punishment for her folly in being trapped into having dinner with Neil Saxton. It was just gone seven when she returned to the house. Her bedroom wasn't the largest of the upstairs rooms, but as far as she was concerned it had the best view. Its tiny dormer window looked out on to fields and, beyond them, the hills of the Cheviot countryside. It was a view of which she never grew tired or bored and, as she stood by the window breathing in the fresh coolness of the early evening air, she reflected on how very fortunate she had been that fate had stepped in just in time, allowing her to salvage this cottage and its land from the destruction of her father's estate.

What she had not known about Julian at the time she married him was that, not only did he not love her, but he was also an inveterate gambler. He had married her quite cold-bloodedly, seeing her fortune as his only means of paying off his even then huge gambling debts, and once having paid them off he had gone on to gamble away not only all her father's careful investments, but every single asset that Rue had been left—and she had known nothing at all about it.

It had been shocking enough to learn about his death, even though by then they had been living apart for five of the six months of their marriage.

That another woman had been driving the car in which they had died had not really come as any surprise to her. He had made it more than plain to her, after that one appalling night of their honeymoon, just how inadequate he found her as a woman, and she had been left in no doubt as to his intentions to replace her in his bed.

Battered and bruised physically as well as emotionally, her dreams and illusions totally destroyed, she had only been able to feel relief that she would not be called upon to suffer his physical assault on her again. The discovery that the papers he had asked her to sign in the days leading up to their marriage had in fact been the power of attorney which gave him total control of her fortune had meant nothing at all to her until her solicitor had worriedly and uncomfortably explained that not only was she now a widow, but she was also completely penniless and her home, Parnham Court, would have to be sold in order to meet all of her husband's gambling debts. And then, right at the last moment, when she was just about to sign the documents handing Parnham Court over, her solicitor had discovered the possibility of transferring to herself in her own name the freehold of Vine Cottage and its land, under an obscure legal loophole caused by the fact that at one time the cottage and its land had been made over to the gardener.

At first the cottage had simply been a place to live, somewhere to hide away, but as the months had gone by she had found herself growing attached to it, loving it, so that now it was part of her in a way that Parnham Court had never been.

Her father had bought the Court on his marriage to her mother, a gift to his new young wife, and he had kept the house on after her death as a home for himself and his motherless child. He had run his business from the Court and had even set up a laboratory there so that he could enjoy the research on which his fortune had originally been founded.

The patent for the drug he had discovered had run out shortly after his death, so that even funds from that source were no longer available to Rue. For a girl who had never known anything but the comforts of expensive wealth, poverty had come as a shock. But there were degrees of poverty, as Rue was the first to admit, just as she was the first to admit that it was far easier to be poor in the countryside than it was in one of the stark, lonely tower blocks of the country's inner cities.

She had discovered within herself a strength that she had never suspected could exist, and with it had come a certain peace of mind. Not that she would ever be able to forgive herself for her folly in being taken in by Julian. The young girl she had once been was so alien to her now that she could scarcely comprehend that she and that girl were one and the same person.

She showered in the bathroom off her bedroom, turning quickly away as she caught a glimpse of her nude body in the mirror. Her own nudity was something she had felt slightly uncomfortable with ever since the first night of her honeymoon, when Julian had looked down at her as she lay, shocked and exhausted, on the hotel bed, and told her cruelly just how deficient he found her as a woman.

It was not that there was anything specifically wrong with her shape. She was small, it was true, very narrow on the hips and the waist, with full, soft breasts that she was at great pains to disguise with heavy sweaters and loose T-shirts. No, her abhorrence of her body was caused more by its inward flaws than any outward failings.

Even now sometimes, at night, she dreamt she could hear Julian's mocking laughter as she wept and begged him not to touch her. Before their marriage he had been so gentle, so caring, so tender, so very much the considerate lover. She ought to have realised it was all simply a ploy, a façade, but she had been too thrilled and excited by his declarations of love, too eager to believe that he desired her to ever imagine that he was lying.

She had deserved to be hurt, she told herself ruthlessly, towelling her body dry with rough ferocity until her skin glowed a bright peach. Her sexuality was not something she ever allowed herself to think about these days. When she was in the company of other women she listened to their frank exchanges regarding their lovers' prowess or lack of it and sometimes their even franker descriptions of their own needs and desires, and, although she smiled and laughed and made the appropriate comments, inside her body felt dead. They may as well have been speaking in a foreign language when they described their pleasure, so different was her own experience.

She had never experienced sexual pleasure other than fleetingly and tenuously in those early days of their courtship, when Julian had teased her with kisses that promised so much and yet in the end meant so very little. Perhaps if she had not been so sheltered, so naïve, she might have realised the truth, might have queried the sincerity of a man who professed to desire her and yet at the same time seemed content with no more than a good-night kiss.

It had not been with desire that he had come to her on their wedding night but with rage and resentment, and with a determination to let her know exactly what role she was to play in his life. He had entered her brutally and ruthlessly, without making any attempt to prepare her for his possession, taking an almost sadistic satisfaction in her pain and shock, and then, when she had cried out, he had punished her for it, inflicting bruises and contusions on her pale skin which had taken days to heal.

After that first night he had never come back to her bed, and she had been too relieved to care. In that one short night he had ripped away the veils of innocence and naïveté which had protected her, and she had seen all that her marriage was going to be. She had lived in a state of shock after that, relieved that he continued to stay away from Parnham Court and yet at the same time too proud to seek advice from those who might have been able to help and advise her.

His death had brought about her release in more ways than one, and she had not been able to mourn for him. Now she was a different woman from that naïve, foolish nineteen-year-old girl. Now she reflected hardily that she was better off for what had happened to her, and her life as it was now was richer in all the things that mattered than it had ever been when she was her father's pampered heiress.

She had no regrets about the loss of her father's wealth, other than those that sprang from guilt caused by her knowledge that there were many, many needy causes that could have benefited from her inheritance. For herself, she was content as she was, and proud of her own small achievements and the progress she had made towards independence.

It was true, as her solicitor had warned her only this morning, that a bad summer, a freak thunderstorm, anything, in fact, that damaged her flower-crop, could jeopardise her financial position almost disastrously. She had very little money behind her. All the profits she had made so far had been ploughed straight back into the business and, although it was true that she had neither mortgage nor debts to worry about, she still had to live.

She pulled on her housecoat. It had been one of her father's last Christmas gifts to her, worn and faded now but still comfortable and warm, even if it was a trifle girlish for a woman of twenty-five. There were very few clothes in her wardrobe. The expensive designer things she had bought as a teenager had either been sold or given away, most of them too outrageous to last for more than one fashion season. In the place of the silks and satins she had once worn, she now wore denim jeans and cotton sweatshirts—hardly the sort of thing one could put on for dinner with a man like Neil Saxton, she reflected wryly as she opened her wardrobe doors and checked abruptly.

Why should it matter what she wore? She had no desire to impress the man. Women adorned their bodies in silks and satins so that they would be pleasing to the male of the species, she reminded herself grimly. She had no desire to please the eye or the sexual appetite of any man.

She reached out for a pair of clean jeans and then hesitated, her pride, that same pride that had driven her to accept his invitation in the first place, making her check and turn instead to frown over the few formal clothes she possessed. There were a couple of suits, the one she had worn this morning and a heavier, more winter-weight one, which she wore for important business meetings with her bank manager or her accountant.

There was her raincoat, a classically cut trench-coat in a waterproof stone-coloured fabric, and a heavy navy winter coat she had splurged out on and bought for herself the previous winter. There were a couple of tailored linen dresses she had bought in a second-hand clothes shop which would have been eminently suitable for city shopping on a hot day, but were hardly the right sort of things to go out for dinner in, and then there were her two evening dresses. One was full-length and formal, and she kept that for the rare winter balls she was obliged to attend; the other—she reached out towards it, and then tensed—the other had been a gift from a client for whom she had done rather a lot of work.

Hannah Ford and her husband had moved into the area less than eighteen months ago. Originally from London, Tom Ford had been forced by ill-health to take a fresh look at his life-style. He had been a successful investment manager in the high-pressure field of corporate finance, but one heart attack and a threatened bypass operation had been enough to suggest to his employers that they should give him a sideways move to a country branch of his bank. Hannah, whose career as an interior designer was just beginning to take off, had given up her own work to come with him, and the move had paid off for them in more ways than one.

Determined not to allow him to feel guilty over the fact that she had given up a very promising post, Hannah had insisted on starting up in business on her own. Even she admitted that she was astounded by her own success. In fact, she had been so successful that Tom was now thinking of giving up his bank job completely so that he could handle the financial side of her business. As if that had not been enough, within six months of moving to the Cheviots Hannah had discovered that she was pregnant.

As she'd confided to Rue, at thirty-nine the last thing she wanted was to start a family, but, once Lucy Saffron Ford had arrived, no parents could have been more doting or adoring than Hannah and Tom, and Hannah was even talking about providing Lucy with a brother or a sister. Having seen one of Rue's beautifully arranged baskets in the home of one of her clients, Hannah had lost no time in getting in touch with Rue and asking her to design some arrangements to complement her own colour-schemes.

Astounded by the very modest fee Rue had asked, ridiculously low by London standards, or so Hannah had told her, she had presented Rue at Christmas with a beautifully wrapped, large box. Inside it, beneath layer upon layer of white tissue paper, had been a dress like no other Rue had ever seen. It had been designed by a friend of hers, especially for Rue, Hannah had told her.

It was black velvet, the softest black velvet Rue had ever seen, and cut so plainly yet so cleverly that it was only when it was actually on that the skill of its designer could truly be seen. The long-sleeved bodice moulded Rue's soft curves and tiny waist; the slightly gathered tulip-shaped skirt skimmed her knees and hinted at the fragile curve of her hips; the ruffled bustle at the back added emphasis to the skirt and a formal touch to the dress, which drew everyone's eyes to her whenever Rue wore it. She had told Hannah initially that the dress simply wasn't her and at any rate was far too expensive a gift, but Hannah had looked so crestfallen, so hurt, that Rue had not been able to refuse to accept it.

Hannah had had a party on New Year's Eve and she had insisted that Rue wear the dress then. Rue had done, but despite the many flattering comments she had received from Hannah's male guests she had not really been deceived. Men flattered and paid compliments because they wanted something; their words meant nothing and were not to be taken seriously, and so she had held them at bay with a cool, assessing smile and an indifference which made Hannah, who was watching her, sigh with exasperation.

She knew nothing of Rue's past other than that she had been unhappily married and was now a widow. She knew of Rue's connection with Parnham Court from village gossip, but she was not the kind of woman to press for confidences that were not freely given, and she respected Rue's right to her privacy, even while she deplored her friend's determination to live her life completely excluding any members of the male sex, apart from the faithful Horatio.

Rue lifted the dress out of the wardrobe and held it against her. With her hair scraped back in a ponytail, and her nose peeling a little from sunburn, she was hardly the type of woman most suited to wearing such a very seductively sophisticated dress. She half made to put it back in the wardrobe, and then she remembered the way Neil Saxton had looked at her the first time they met. Before she knew quite what she was doing, she was putting on fresh underwear and zipping the dress closed.

She had never worn heavy make-up, and after she had brushed her damp hair into place she applied a hint of blusher to her cheeks and eye-shadow to her lids before coating her mouth with soft pink lipstick. Once she had finished, she eyed her reflection dispassionately, seeing only the woman that Julian had told her that she was—unfeminine, sexless, inadequate—not knowing that it was *his* inadequacy that had led to his cruelty to her.

She was half-way downstairs when she suddenly wondered what on earth she was doing and why she had dressed up to have dinner with Neil Saxton. She turned on the stairs, swiftly starting to unzip her dress as she did so. But it was too late.

In the kitchen Horatio growled and then barked, and as she stood there, frozen with indecision, she heard the front door clang. She had a moment's cowardly impulse to stay where she was and simply hope that he would eventually get tired of waiting and go away, but as quickly as the thought formed she realised the idiocy of it and instead turned back reluctantly and went downstairs.

The stairs were to one side of the house, narrow and deeply angled and coming down into a tiny inner hallway. From there she walked through her study and opened the door into the narrow hall. It was still light outside, although because of the cottage's tiny windows it was necessary for her to have the lights on inside.

Perhaps that was why Neil Saxton suddenly seemed so much taller than she remembered, she thought as she opened the door to him and he stooped to walk into the tiny hallway. It was barely big enough for one person, never mind two, and Rue found her body tensing as she caught the clear, fresh scent of his skin, faintly mixed with the cologne she recognised as the one he had worn before.

Like her, he had changed, and it came as rather a shock to discover that he was wearing a formal dinner-suit. Anger followed the shock. Had he hoped to intimidate and embarrass her by dressing so formally? Unaware that her feelings showed in a brilliant flash of her eyes as she looked directly at him, she heard him catch his breath lightly and focus on her.

Immediately her anger turned to suspicion as she read what she knew could only be pseudo-admiration in his eyes.

'I'll just put Horatio in the kitchen,' she told him. 'If you'd like to wait outside for me...'

'Why?' he asked her blandly. 'Surely you aren't frightened of being alone with me?'

His mockery annoyed her, all the more so because she suspected that he did actually know how very uneasy she was in his company.

'Hardly,' she told him crisply. 'It's just that this door only locks from the inside.'

He looked at the lock on the door and she saw him frown slightly.

'You should have a safety chain put on this,' he told her curtly, and than added, 'You're very isolated here. Don't you ever feel afraid?'

Rue's chin tilted.

'No,' she told him shortly, wondering what he would say if she told him her fears were all inner ones, fear of herself, of her own inadequacies and failings, rather than of the world outside. Failings of a type that this man probably never imagined could exist.

'Mmm...' he said thoughtfully. 'You surprise me, a woman living on your own. I should have thought you would be a little bit more security-conscious.'

For some reason his words made a fine tremor of apprehension clench her body, and she said huskily to him, 'Perhaps in future I shall be.'

She opened the door and held on to it until he had stepped back outside, firmly locking it behind him and then taking Horatio into the kitchen. Having locked the door and then checked it, Rue made her way round to the front of the house.

She gave a faint start as she realised that Neil was waiting for her on the front path. She had expected him to go straight to his car, and it was very unnerving to walk down the path knowing that he was there, two paces behind her. For some reason she could not fathom, his presence made her feel uneasy and threatened in a way that had nothing to do with the residual dislike of his sex which had been Julian's bequest to her.

She had to wait while he unlocked his car door and, to her surprise, once he had freed the central locking system, he came round to the passenger door and opened it for her, not mockingly or teasingly, but so simply and automatically that she realised that it was an action he would perform for any member of her sex, no matter what her age or appearance.

As she gave him a stiff, 'Thank you,' his eyebrows quirked and as he looked down at her he said,

'Ah, I see I have offended you, although why good manners should ever be offensive I'm afraid I'm at a loss to understand.'

Rue wanted to make some clever comment about his treatment of her as though she were incapable of opening the car door for herself being both demeaning and derogatory, but somehow or other the words simply would not form. In the past she had taken it as her due that men should open doors for her and generally protect and pamper her, but that had been before she realised what lay behind such paternalistic patronage.

And yet her body trembled slightly as she recognised her own weakness and was forced to admit that there was something very pleasant about being treated as though her comfort was of importance. Remember he wants your land, she warned herself, as she slammed the door closed and Neil came round to slide into the driver's seat next to her.

That was what all this was about, no matter how much he might try to pretend otherwise: he aimed to flatter and coax her into a state of vulnerability by trying to conceal his real motives. A man of his means could obtain as many dried flower arrangements as he wished from anywhere without having to go to the necessity of entertaining a woman whose company and person could only bore him. No, the reason he had invited her to dinner was nothing to do with his desire to have her advice about suitable floral arrangements for his mother's visit; he just wanted to soften her up so that he could get her to part with her land.

She tugged impatiently on the seat-belt and then frowned down at it as it refused to move. Next to her Neil pulled firmly on his and was just about to push the catch into the socket when he realised what had happened. He let his go and reached across her. As his head and torso filled the small space between her and the windscreen, Rue automatically tensed, fear making her blood run cold through her veins, her breath locked in her throat as she fought down the panic rising swiftly inside her.

'It's quite easy,' Neil was saying calmly, 'you just hold it like this and pull gently.'

Rue sat rigidly in her seat, arching her spine back against it, her stomach quivering with anxiety as Neil pulled the seat-belt across it and secured it to her side. He was so close to her that she could see the tiny lines fanning out from his eyes and the hard, masculine texture of his skin. She could see also the dark line of his shaven beard along his jaw and over his upper lip.

'What's wrong?'

The quiet question startled her. She had been lost in the bewildering discovery that, close to, the apparent hardness of his face was softened by the fullness of his bottom lip.

'I... nothing,' she floundered, desperately conscious of how odd her behaviour must appear.

'There. I think you'll find that's secure now,' he told her, tugging gently on the seat-belt and then straightening up to fasten his own. As he did so, he asked her quietly, 'Am I so very like him?'

She had been fiddling with the clasp of her handbag, but now it fell nervously from her fingers and she stared at him, unable to control or conceal her reaction.

'I... what do you mean?' she asked him.

The smile he gave her made her shiver.

'Come on, Rue. I wasn't born yesterday,' he told her grittily. 'Ever since we've met you've been treating me as you might a rabid dog. Since as far as I know I haven't done anything to merit such treatment, the only other explanation that comes to mind is that I must remind you of someone who does.'

'Julian... Julian was fair,' she told him, huskily and truthfully, and out of the corner of her eye she saw him frown as though her words were not the ones he had wanted to hear. But then, what man ever liked having his judgement questioned? He was wrong if he thought that he in any way resembled her late husband.

Julian had not been overly tall; about five foot ten. He had been fair-haired and blue-eyed. There had been something almost film-star-like in his boyish looks, whereas Neil had far too hard-boned and masculine a countenance to ever be called good-looking. But yet there was a resemblance, a connection. Not in the way that Neil looked, but in the reaction his presence caused her; in the very definite *frisson* of sensation that touched her nerve-endings whenever he came too close to her.

It was the same *frisson* she had experienced in those early heady days when she was first falling in love with Julian. She shuddered, inwardly terrified by what she was admitting. It had been desire for Julian that had caused that sensation, but it was fear and dislike of Neil that was bringing it back. It had to be. It was impossible for her to desire any man, but most especially this one, who had made it plain he would go to any lengths in order to obtain her land. Though she could understand why.

As long as somebody else owned it, he would be vulnerable to the possibility that they might sell it to a speculator, much like the builder who had approached her. Someone who would use her few acres to build an estate of houses which would encroach almost half-way down the drive which led to Parnham Court, which would ruin the outlook from those magnificent second-floor windows, which would destroy the house's exclusivity, and bring down its commercial value considerably. Oh, yes, she could understand why he wanted her land, but she still wasn't going to sell it to him; to him or to anyone else. It meant far too much to her.

She had been a fool to accept this invitation, to lay herself open to the tactics he would obviously try to use against her. Once he knew she was vulnerable to him... She shut off the thoughts, relieved to discover the car had come to a halt, and that they were parked outside the main entrance to the house.

As he had done before, Neil came round to open her car door for her, but this time she was ready for him and wrenched the handle open before he could touch it, almost stumbling in her haste to get out of the car. The look he gave her made her face burn, but she told herself stubbornly that she had every right to protect herself from him, that he was only trying to charm and deceive her.

He escorted her into the house which had once been so familiar to her. Inside, the large hallway very little had changed. She had been lucky enough to find a buyer who had wanted to purchase most of the furnishings in addition to the building and land itself, and as she walked into the hall she recognised that some of them at least were still here.

The graceful staircase curled upwards to the second and third storeys in a delicate spiral. Three flights above them the painted dome of the ceiling with its allegorical Biblical fresco was still as awesomely eye-catching as it had always been. The large oval hallway, with its black and white lozenge-tiled floor, felt chilly after the warmth of the car. Four pairs of huge mahogany doors led off it, and between them, on either side of the wall, matching gilt rococo mirrors and tables. A huge crystal chandelier illuminated this hallway, and Neil reached out and switched it on, brilliant prisms of light glittering sharply, so much so that it almost hurt Rue's eyes.

'This way,' Neil told her, touching her shoulder and making her jump as he indicated the first pair of double doors.

Rue hesitated a little, since she knew that they led not into the dining-room but into the library, and from there into the small private sitting-room which she and her father had almost always used. Off the sitting-room was the conservatory, and she discovered, as Neil led her into it, that it was here that they were going to eat.

'The dining-room, beautiful though it is, is hardly conducive to a small, intimate dinner,' he told her, correctly interpreting her surprise.

He offered her a drink, and when she shook her head in refusal he explained that, while everything was ready, it would take him a few minutes to serve the meal. Rue didn't really care how long it would take him. With every second that passed she was regretting more and more her folly in ever agreeing to come here. The very last thing she wanted was to sit down and eat with this man, and yet when Neil returned, pushing a heated trolley in front of him, the rich, tempting aroma of the food reminded her how long it had been since she had last eaten.

Meals during the summer were snatched affairs at the best of times, and today, for one reason or another, she had managed to miss out on both lunch and the snack she normally ate around five o'clock.

'After we've eaten I'll show you the suite of rooms I'm thinking of furnishing for my mother,' Neil told her as he served their main course.

Their starter had been a delicious concoction of fresh salmon delicately flavoured with herbs, which

Rue had found mouthwateringly good. She had complimented him stiffly on it and had burned with inner anger as she sensed his amusement.

She hated the thought that he might be laughing at her, even while she acknowledged that his amusement was probably richly deserved. They had almost finished their main course when he suddenly asked her out of the blue, 'Tell me a bit more about this husband of yours. Why did you marry him in the first place?'

Rue had just taken a mouthful of wine and she almost choked on it, unable to believe what she was hearing.

'What exactly is it you want to know?' she asked him tightly, letting him see her anger. 'Why he wanted to marry me? Surely that's self-evident: I was very rich and very stupid.'

'You were also very young and criminally unprotected,' Neil cut in drily, adding, 'Don't take all the blame for what happened on your shoulders, Rue.'

She was astounded by his arrogance, and the anger and fear she had suppressed so successfully during their meal suddenly resurfaced. She stood up furiously, pushing her plate away from her.

'You're wasting your time, Neil,' she told him boldly. 'I know exactly why you've brought me here on this pretext of wanting my advice.'

He had stood up too, moving away from the table at the same moment as she did, and effectively blocking her exit. The conservatory wasn't a very large room and the plants that crowded it made it seem even smaller, claustrophobically so, or so it seemed to Rue, her skin suddenly too tight and hot.

Panic started to course through her. As he came towards her, she had heard Neil saying grittingly, 'Do you, now? Well, then, it won't surprise you if I do this, will it?' And before she could evade him he had taken hold of her and lowered his mouth to hers, silencing her furious words of protest, smothering them beneath the fierce pressure of his lips.

It was a hard, angry kiss that left her in no doubt as to his contempt and dislike of her. As she fought to break free of him its pressure deepened and, unbelievably, just as panic started to claw at her, the pressure softened and became coaxing rather than punitive, his hands caressing on her skin rather than imprisoning.

Too bemused to break free, Rue stood completely immobile as Neil made a soft sound against her mouth, gathering her even closer. Then, as his lips feathered softly against her own, her sanity abruptly reasserted itself and she pulled away from him, furious with him and furious with herself.

'I hope you don't expect me to apologise for that,' Neil told her as he let her go.

'How dare you?' Rue demanded rawly, ignoring his comment. 'How dare you stand there and say that to me...?' Unexpectedly, tears welled in her eyes, and she turned away from him, shaking from head to foot. 'What have I said or done that made you think I would welcome an...an attack like that?'

'An attack? It wasn't like that... I was angry, yes...'

'Angry...' Rue whirled round and faced him, her eyes glittering with unshed tears. 'And that anger

gave you the right to—force yourself on me, did
it? To... Oh, you men are all the same. You think
you have the God-given right to punish us...to
discipline us by forcing yourselves on us. You
brought me here tonight so that you could persuade me to sell you my land, and then, when you
realised it wasn't going to work, you thought you'd
use a different means of persuasion. My husband
was just like you,' she flung bitterly at him. 'He
punished me by...' She broke off suddenly, to stare
at him as she caught the expression of angry disgust
darkening his eyes.

'I don't believe I'm hearing any of this,' he told
her tersely. 'I kissed you for one reason only, Rue,
and that had nothing to do with any pre-planned
Machiavellian plot to get you to part with your land.
The reason I kissed you was simply because I've
been wanting to do so ever since I set eyes on you.
All right, so it shouldn't have happened the way it
did, and for that I *do* apologise...but to accuse
me of...' He looked at her and asked quietly, 'What
were you accusing me of, Rue? I *think* I know, but
I'm not sure I can believe what I'm hearing. I think
I can understand how you feel about your
husband—he obviously gave you a bad time both
in bed and out of it—but there must have been other
men since who've shown you that all men *aren't*
the same...' He caught his breath, his eyes narrowing, a dark flush of colour burning shockingly
along his cheekbones as he realised the truth. 'There
haven't been any other men, have there?' he demanded flatly and very quietly.

If he had made the slightest move towards her, Rue knew she would have turned and fled, but because he stayed where he was, because her emotions were in such a disorientated and thoroughly confused state already, she simply stood and stared at him, unable to deny his words with what they both knew would be a lie.

'What did he do to you, Rue?' he asked softly. 'What in *hell* did he do to make you feel that every man who touches you wants to hurt you? That *is* how you feel, isn't it?' he persisted.

'I don't want to talk about it,' Rue told him lightly, dragging air into her tormented lungs, her body so weak with shock and anxiety that she could barely stand. 'I want to go home. Now. I must go home...' Suddenly she was gabbling meaningless phrases and words, or so it sounded to her own ears, her voice rising high with panic and pain. She half stumbled and half ran towards the door, but Neil got there before her.

'Let me go,' she demanded frantically, only to realise that he wasn't touching her at all, her face burning as she saw the pity and the sympathy in his eyes. But they weren't real, she told herself; they were just a trap... just a ruse... just part of his plan to get her to sell her land to him.

'I'm not letting you go like this. All right,' he told her, 'I'll take you home if that's what you want... but I'm not letting you walk out of here alone in this state. In fact, I'm not sure I ought to let you go at all,' he added under his breath.

'You can't stop me,' Rue protested feebly, struggling to regain her self-control, and as though he sensed her panic he stayed scrupulously away from her, watching her with eyes that registered every tiny nuance of emotion that crossed her face.

As he looked at her, he was torn between pity and anger. He had sensed her hostility right from the first moment he saw her, but that had not stopped him feeling desire for her.

As he escorted her out to his car she threw at him, 'It doesn't matter what you do or say—I'll *never* sell my land to you.'

'Never is one hell of a long time,' he reminded her as he started the engine and switched on the lights. 'And when I want something, I don't give up until I've got it.'

CHAPTER FOUR

SEVERAL times during the night Rue woke up disturbed by uneasy dreams which left her feeling anxious and on edge and somehow very alone, despite the comforting noises Horatio made in his sleep. Eventually, at half-past three, knowing she wasn't going to be able to get back to sleep, she got up and went downstairs. Hands clasped around a comforting mug of coffee, she stared out of the window into the greyness of the pre-dawn sky.

She wasn't used to feeling ill at ease with herself this way. Although she had never forgotten the trauma of her short marriage, she had forced herself to put it behind her. The life she had built for herself here in Vine Cottage was secure and comfortable. Other people might consider her life lonely and indeed in some ways unnatural for a young woman of her age, but to Rue that loneliness represented safety.

If there was no one to share her life with her, then there was no one to hurt her, and she had been quite content for it to be that way. Her friends did occasionally try their hand at matchmaking, but she always left the men concerned in no doubt at all as to her feelings, so that very few of them were brave enough to risk getting a second rebuff. And now, shockingly, within a very short space of time Neil Saxton had invaded her life, threatening her security in a way that made her feel bitterly resentful.

Last night, when he had kissed her... She shivered and put down her half-empty cup of coffee. She didn't want to think about that kiss... about the sensation that had touched her so very briefly and so very unforgettably, before she had torn herself out of his arms.

Irritated with herself for her weakness, she reached out and switched on the radio, tuning in to the farmers' weather forecast. Worry darkened her eyes as she listened to the bulletin. It was warning that the spell of good weather was almost at an end, and that thunderstorms were on their way.

Her main crop of summer-flowering blossoms needed another two days of sunshine at least before they would be at their peak. If she picked them before then, the blooms would not be open to their fullest extent, but if she left them and the thunderstorms arrived early... Gnawing on her bottom lip, she refilled her mug, roaming restlessly round the kitchen and then going to stand in front of the window.

It was getting properly light now. The herbs she grew in the shelter of the walled garden were always safe from high winds and need not cause her too much concern, but her fields lay beyond the protection of the walls and were too exposed.

The majority of the plants she grew for drying were summer-flowering. It was then that the rich colours that were so popular with her clients were at their best. If she lost that crop... She shivered, her shoulders sagging slightly.

It was at times like this that she was truly conscious of being alone, of wanting... What? she derided herself angrily. A shoulder to lean on? Immediately a mental image of Neil Saxton flashed across her mind. Angrily she dismissed it, furious with the way her body was playing tricks with her. The man was her enemy. He wanted her land, and if she was stupid enough to fall for his curious charm and flattery then she fully deserved the fate that would undoubtedly be hers.

Hadn't she learnt anything from her marriage to Julian? Hadn't she sworn after he had left her that she would never, ever again allow any man to gain an ascendency over her through her emotions? And yet here she was, in a moment of tiredness and weakness, allowing herself to give in to the basic feminine urge to seek protection from life's harshness—and why? Wasn't it true that women were and had to be far more emotionally strong than men, that women all over the world had to cope with far worse than she was having to endure? Many, many millions of them had not only to earn their own living, but to bring up children as well, often without the support of the man who had fathered them.

Hadn't she learnt yet that men were not to be trusted, that it was far, far better to remain independent? The weather bulletin finished and music echoed from the radio. Impatiently she reached out and switched it off.

Horatio came padding into the kitchen and looked enquiringly and a little disapprovingly at her, as though to ask what on earth she was doing out of bed at such an early hour. It was too late to go back to sleep—another hour and it would be fully light. She was impatient suddenly to be out in the fields, checking on the progress of her flowers, even as she acknowledged that no amount of willing them to be ready was going to have the slightest effect upon them.

Upstairs she showered and dressed, pulling on a pair of clean but very old jeans and a thin T-shirt. It had faded and shrunk in the wash, and clung a little too closely to the curve of her breasts for her liking. She shrugged the thought aside as she pulled on a sweatshirt for extra warmth. After all, no one was likely to see her in it.

As soon as it was properly light, she went into the field. It was too early as yet to check on the progress of her flowers. They needed the sun to warm them before she would be able to do that. Restless and yet tired at the same time, she went into the barn and started preparing the blossoms she had picked the previous day for drying. As always, once she started work she became totally absorbed in what she was doing, so much so that Horatio's soft whine of pleasure and recognition didn't break through her fierce concentration until it was too late.

A shadow fell across the doorway, momentarily blocking out the early sun. She lifted her head, tension quivering sharply in her stomach as she recognised her visitor.

'What do you want?' she demanded shortly, her whole body stiff with rejection and fear.

She saw his eyebrows lift, hating the amusement that crinkled his eyes as he bent down to fuss Horatio. To the dog he said thoughtfully, 'It seems that your mistress is not in a very good mood this morning. Now, I wonder why.'

The look he gave her made her face burn. Mentally seething, Rue turned her face away from him. How very like a man to assume that just because she had not welcomed him with open arms last night she must now be suffering from regrets and sexual frustration.

'Why have you come here?' she demanded fiercely. 'If it's about the land, I've already told you . . .'

'It isn't about the land,' he interrupted her calmly. 'I wanted to talk to you about last night.'

Her eyes betrayed her instantly, darkening with apprehension and fear. He reached out a hand to touch her and then, as though he had thought better of it, let it drop to his side.

'There is nothing to talk about,' she told him stiffly. If only he would go away, but he was far too big, far too male for her to be able to force him to do so. Men liked using their physical superiority to dominate women, she thought bitterly. She had learned that from Julian.

'You're trespassing,' she added shortly, and out of the corner of her eyes she saw his mouth harden a little.

'Why is it that you're so antagonistic towards me?' he asked her quietly.

His arrogance and effrontery almost took her breath away. She turned on him, putting down the flowers she had been holding, her hands balled into small fists at her side as she told him fiercely, 'I should have thought you would have the intelligence to know the answer to that! You come here pestering me to sell you my land, even when I've already told you I have no intention of doing so; you invite me to your house under false pretenses and then, when everything else has failed, you try to provoke me into giving you what you want by using the kind of caveman tactics that...'

'Now just a minute,' he interrupted her smoothly. 'Granted, I wanted to buy your land, and I wouldn't be much of a negotiator if I gave up at the first hurdle, but you're completely wrong about what happened last night. You're using your antagonism to mask your fear,' he told her, stunning her with his perception. 'Is it just me who terrifies you so much, I wonder, or is it men in general?'

Rue stared at him without saying a word. She couldn't have said a word. Her throat muscles felt as though they were completely paralysed, her legs so jelly-like with shock that she had to grab hold of the counter to support herself. He was looking right at her, and the calm steadiness of his gaze wouldn't allow her to look away.

He was mesmerising her, Rue thought disjointedly. He was trying to weaken her, to read her mind, to overwhelm her with his maleness in the same way that Julian had once done. It seemed a lifetime before he relented and allowed her to look away, and almost miraculously, as she did so, her throat muscles relaxed and she was able to deny huskily, 'I'm not frightened of you.'

'No?' He said it grimly rather than triumphantly, and then took a step towards her.

Instinctively Rue moved back until she felt the hard spikes of the worktop against her spine.

'Lie to me if you want to, Rue,' he told her sardonically, watching her, 'but don't lie to yourself.'

'I'm not,' Rue fibbed. 'Oh, I know you want me to be frightened of you. You want to panic me into selling my land. I know what kind of man you are. You're just like Julian.'

He moved so swiftly that she didn't have time to escape, hemming her in with the bulk and heat of his body as he leaned towards her, resting his hands either side of her on the worktop, so that there was simply no way she could escape.

'I'm getting a little tired of being told I'm like your husband. Hardly a flattering comparison, is it? Is it?' he demanded brutally when she refused to speak. 'Or is it just that, to you, *all* men are like him, Rue?'

The sudden softness in his voice had the most peculiar effect upon her. Her throat suddenly seemed painfully raw, her chest tight with what, if she hadn't known better, she might have thought to be unshed tears. Even her eyes felt dry and gritty, and she had to resist the urge to rub them like a little girl.

'I'm sorry about what he did to you,' Neil continued in an even gentler voice. 'He obviously hurt you monstrously, both physically and emotionally. I won't deny that there are men like that, but I'm not one of them,' he told her, his voice suddenly starting to harden, 'and if you can't tell that for yourself, then perhaps it's time that someone taught you just how to recognise that difference.'

'I don't need teaching anything,' Rue flared at him, frightened by the weakness she had experienced at that momentary softening of his tone, that had made her ache inside in a way that was completely unfamiliar to her. It had made her yearn to reach out to him, to soak up the warmth and strength of him. It had shown her a terrifying vulnerability in herself that she had never dreamed existed, and she fought against it like a terrified animal caught in a trap.

'You think not?' he said, and suddenly his voice was a sensual purr, as his glance dropped to her mouth. Appallingly, Rue felt it start to tremble. His glance seared her almost as much as the pressure of his mouth had done the previous night. She wanted to thrust him away from her and escape from his presence, but she was terrified of what might happen if she risked any physical contact between them.

'I came here this morning to apologise for having frightened you last night,' he told her, shocking her into immobility, 'and to remind you that you still haven't given me your advice about my mother's rooms.'

Rue could hardly believe her ears. Did he really have the gall to imagine that she would fall for that stupid fiction a second time?

'I'm afraid I've far too many commitments on at the moment to do anything like that,' she told him coldly. 'What you really need, anyway, is an interior designer. I can recommend a good local one.'

She turned her back on him and looked on the desk for the pad and pen she always kept at hand. The sensation of him standing so close behind her made tension prickle down her spine. She wrote out Hannah's address and telephone number and turned back to him, almost thrusting it at him. He took it from her and said in an ominously calm voice, 'You know, I wouldn't have thought you were a coward, Rue.'

'A coward?' Her eyes flashed fire and resentment. 'I'm not.'

'Oh, yes, you are,' he told her softly. 'You are a coward who's terrified of facing up to reality, to life, and that's why you're clinging so desperately to this cottage and this land. Without it you'd be like a tortoise without its shell.'

'No, that's not true!' Rue flung at him, and Horatio, sensing her distress, started to whine.

'You realise, don't you, that it can be just as dangerous to isolate yourself from the rest of humanity as it can be to risk emotional pain through contact with it?' His voice held a warning that made her tense and look at him.

He had asked her once already if she didn't find the isolation of the cottage frightening. She had told him no, and that had been the truth, but now suddenly a quiver of apprehension shot through her.

'I'm in no danger here,' she told him unequivocally.

He looked at her for a long time and then replied drily, 'If you really think that, you're even more unworldly than I had already supposed. Be careful you don't play Sleeping Beauty for too long, Rue,' he warned her, as he stepped away from her and walked towards the door. 'When you eventually want to wake up, you might find it's too late.'

He had gone before she could make any retort. She remained where she was for another half-hour, but her concentration on her task was broken. Every few minutes her normally nimble fingers would suddenly still and she would realise with a sudden pang of fear that she was standing staring into nothing, her mind so totally preoccupied with Neil Saxton that she was hardly even aware of her surroundings.

Impatient and angry with herself, she collected Horatio and set out for the field. The hot summer sun had long since dried the early morning mist off the blooms, and her flowers were enjoying the heat of the sun with an almost sensual appreciation.

She touched the velvety petals of a midnight blue larkspur, wondering why she had never noticed before this almost wanton drinking up of the sun's heat. Until Neil Saxton had forced his way into her life, there had been no necessity for her to have such thoughts. That knowledge made her feel uncomfortable with herself. No matter how much she might wish it, the flowers were still not ready for picking.

There was work she could have done, but for some unaccountable reason she felt too listless to do it. Later on in the afternoon, when the sun started to go, she would have the watering to do, but right now...

On a sudden impulse she headed back to the cottage, opening her fridge/freezer and collecting from it two of the fruit pies she had baked the previous week. She picked some fresh herbs from the garden and, on impulse, a pretty bunch of flowers, and then, telling Horatio that on this occasion he could not go with her, she headed for the back door, carrying a wicker basket full of the things she had collected together.

Her destination was one of the cottages in the row that lined the main street of the village. Her father had bought it for his housekeeper when she retired, and as she got into her car and drove towards the village Rue reflected guiltily that it was almost a month since she had last gone to visit Mrs Dacre. A widow with no family of her own, she had been fond of Rue, and, although she had very good neighbours either side of her in the village, Rue kept as closely in touch with her as she could.

The village was quiet, satiated with heat and sun. Too far off the beaten track to be a tourist attraction, it remained as it had been for almost a hundred years: a jumble of tiny cottages lined either side of the village street, the small front gardens a tumble of pretty flowers. Once these houses had been the homes of the labourers who worked on the large agricultural estate. The plots to the rear of the cottages had once provided a year's supply of vegetables for the labourers' families. Now very few of them were used for that purpose. Most of the occupants were elderly, their families long ago grown-up.

There was very little work in the immediate area, and as Rue parked her car and got out she wondered a little sadly if, once the new motorway system had been completed, the village would simply become another dormitory suburb to the city.

She walked round the back of the row of cottages, knowing from previous experience that Mrs Dacre would be alarmed at the sound of someone knocking at her front door. She found the old lady sitting in a chair in her back garden. Well into her seventies now, she was still very independent, cutting a little when she saw the basket that Rue had brought her.

'I'm afraid my pastry's never going to be as good as yours,' Rue told her with a smile, 'but you were saying the last time I called that you could never be bothered to make a pie just for yourself, and since I was baking anyway...'

'Yes, it's hard to cook just for yourself, when you've been used to doing it for others,' Mrs Dacre told her a little wistfully. 'I miss cooking for your father; he always appreciated his food, Mr Livesey did.'

She saw the look on Rue's face and said a little sharply, 'In my day a girl was brought up to take care of her menfolk, and I don't see anything wrong in that. Of course, I know it's different these days.'

The way she said it, and the expression on her face, suggested that she did not altogether approve of that difference, but Rue coaxed her until the old lady's ruffled feathers were soothed, and she bustled away into her small kitchen to make them both a cup of tea.

Rue listened with half an ear while Mrs Dacre chattered about various village events, her attention wandering a little, until the old lady said sharply, 'So you've got a new neighbour, then? I heard in the post office as how someone new's moved in to the big house. Met him yet, have you?'

'Just briefly,' Rue told her, knowing that the village was probably very well aware of Neil's visit to her, in that unique and almost unfathomable way that villages had of garnering news.

'Mmm... Not married, so I've heard,' Mrs Dacre commented, looking speculatively at Rue.

'I believe not,' Rue said coolly, and then, seeing the look in her late father's housekeeper's eyes, she added firmly, 'He came to see me to ask if I was interested in selling my land.'

'Aye, well, he would want it, wouldn't he,' Mrs Dacre agreed, 'seeing as how it was once part of the estate? Which reminds me, you'll have heard that Bill Jennings has sold off part of his land to that builder who was pestering to buy *your* land from you.'

Bill Jennings owned and farmed what had once been the Court's home farm.

'It's the ten-acre he's sold, so I've heard,' Mrs Dacre continued, and Rue's frown deepened. The ten-acre was in fact several fields, the corner of one of which just touched on the boundary of her own land.

'How will the builder get access to it?' she questioned.

It was true that there was a dirt track to the farm, but that did not give direct access to the piece of land the builder had apparently acquired, and if he actually planned to build there he would surely need some means of access to the main road. Her frown deepened as it suddenly struck her that the easiest way for him to do this would be through Vine Cottage itself.

'He wouldn't be told that he'd bought himself a pig in a poke,' Mrs Dacre continued. 'That land's no use to him as it is. He's no way of getting to and from it, not by road leastways, and Bill's laughing all the way to the bank. Says it's the worst piece of land on the whole farm.'

Rue stayed with the old lady for another half-hour and then, judging that her hostess was beginning to get a little tired, she said her goodbyes and made her way back to her car.

It seemed odd that the builder should have bought that land, inaccessible as it was. He had been furious with her when she had refused to sell him her home and her field, far more furious in many ways than Neil Saxton, she recalled now with a sudden start. And yet she had not felt one tenth of the apprehension and dread she was suffering now.

No, it was not his desire to possess her home and land that intimidated her so much where Neil Saxton was concerned, it was the man himself. Pushing this disturbing thought to the back of her mind, she drove home.

Horatio gave her an ecstatic welcome, bounding at her side as she took him for his walk. When they got back to the cottage the telephone was ringing. Rue picked up the receiver a little reluctantly, only to deride herself for her foolish belief that it must be Neil telephoning her when she heard the voice of her friend Hannah.

'Are you doing anything tonight?' Hannah asked her.

Used to her friend's sudden and impulsive plans, Rue said drily, 'You are joking, aren't you? You do know what time of year this is, I hope?'

'Yes, yes, I know,' Hannah agreed overriding her, 'but surely you can give yourself the odd evening off? You work far too hard, Rue.'

'Look who's talking,' Rue teased her.

'No, seriously,' Hannah intervened, 'how long is it since you've actually had an evening off?'

Rue wondered what her friend would say if she told her the truth, and then wondered again, a little starkly, why it was that she was not telling her friend about Neil's invitation to dinner, or what lay behind it.

'Look, I only want you to come for dinner, and you won't have to stay late. We're doing some business entertaining and I think I'm going to need your support, not to mention the fact that there could be something in it for you.'

'Tell me more,' Rue began, but her friend refused, saying only,

'I can't right now. I'm frantically trying to get the house tidy and something organised for dinner. Just tell me that you'll come.'

With Neil's taunts that she was too isolated from the rest of the human race, too eager to cut herself off from all contact with it, Rue found herself agreeing that she would.

'Eight for eight-thirty, then,' Hannah told her, her voice rising to a scream as Rue heard a resounding crash somewhere in the distance. 'If that's one of my best dinner plates, I'm going to strangle the little monster,' Hannah announced, quickly saying goodbye and replacing the receiver.

Rue was smiling as she put hers down. Despite the fact that at times she claimed she loathed her daughter, Rue knew quite well that Hannah was the most devoted mother, and the little girl was engaging. Rue felt a tiny, disarming tug somewhere in the region of her heart as she remembered how eagerly Hannah's little girl climbed into her own lap and hugged her. There was something about holding the trusting weight of a child in one's arms...

Thoroughly irritated by her own train of thoughts, Rue derided herself for giving in to such sentimentality. If she was going to go out to dinner, she would have to finish the work she had started this morning, which meant at least a couple of hours spent in the drying shed.

Horatio went with her. He accompanied her everywhere if she allowed him to do so, disappearing only occasionally if the lure of the rabbits that populated the Court's parkland proved too much for him. He always returned from these abortive forays out of breath, with a guilty expression in his eyes, almost as though he felt he had to apologise for deserting her.

As the afternoon advanced, the air grew still and hot. Too hot, Rue recognised worriedly. There wasn't a single cloud in the sky, but the sun had taken on a brassy hue which made her suspect that the weather forecast was likely to prove all too correct. She would probably have to spend all day tomorrow picking her flowers whether they were ready or not. Either that or risk losing them altogether if the thunderstorms came early. It was at times like this that she desperately wished she had someone with whom she could share the responsibility and worry of making the right decision.

But there was no one, and as she headed for the drying shed she told herself hardily that she was better off that way.

Having eaten with Mrs Dacre, and knowing full well what an excellent hostess Hannah was, she decided against making a meal, and worked steadily from five until just gone seven, realising suddenly how little time she had in which to get ready. The expensive watering system she had had installed in the spring was now proving its true worth. It was marvellous to be able to go out and ensure, by simply turning on a tap, that her entire crop was watered. Before it had involved backbreaking hours of work, carrying buckets full of water to and from the nearest tap which had been in her walled garden.

The new system had cost a fortune, which was one of the reasons she was so desperately anxious that this season's crop should be a good one. She had perilously little in her bank account. Since Julian's death, money had been a constant source of worry to her, and even though now she didn't have the enormity of Julian's debts to concern her she still suffered from sleepless nights when she lay awake frantically doing sums in her head.

If she lost this summer crop... She wasn't going to lose it, she told herself firmly. The storm wasn't forecast for another two days, which gave her plenty of time to get the blooms in, even if it did mean picking them a little before she would really have wished.

While the sprinkler system was doing its work, she rushed upstairs and hurried into her bathroom. Horatio lay on the floor outside the door and whined protestingly. He knew quite well that she was getting ready to go out and, as always at such times, adopted the manner of an animal who was being ruthlessly abandoned by a heartless owner.

Rue, used to such wiles, firmly ignored them. It was really too hot to wear the black velvet dress, but she had nothing else. It slid easily on to her body, the satin lining stroking her skin, almost like a caress. The thought made her tense and glance quickly over her shoulder, almost as though she half expected Neil Saxton to suddenly materialise at her side.

Damn the man. Why should he have to keep intruding on her thoughts so much?

Half-way through getting changed, the timer which she always set when she was watering went off. Her hair, still slightly damp, curled on to her shoulders and round her face in tiny tendrils, as though glorying in being freed from its normally constraining ponytail. When she was going out, she usually looped it back in a neat twist, considering that long hair left flowing free was for girls under twenty-one, not women of twenty-five, a view she had grimly held on to despite Hannah's astonished laughter when she had passed it on to her.

'You've only got to look at the television to see how many women of over thirty—and over forty—wear their hair long and loose,' Hannah had chided her. 'And yours is so very lovely. You don't know how lucky you are to be so naturally fair.'

Grimly Rue had reiterated that if she had any sense she would have it cut, but at least when it was long it was easy to tie back and keep out of the way.

The evening breeze caught it as she stepped out into the garden, and hurried towards the tap. She didn't see Neil until she had virtually run into him; his hands coming out to steady her made her gasp in shock, her eyes huge and brilliant in the suddenly pale oval of her face. As though her shock was transmitted to him by her flesh, his fingers moved gently on her shoulders, almost as though he was stroking her in reassurance.

'I startled you. I'm sorry, I didn't mean to,' he apologised.

'What are you doing here?' Rue asked him, stepping back from him unwillingly aware of the tiny tremors of sensation racing through her body.

She realised that he was wearing his dinner suit and snapped, 'And if you've come here to try to persuade me to have dinner with you, you're wasting your time. I've got another engagement.'

'I know,' he told her mildly, but Rue could have sworn there was laughter dancing in his eyes. Laughter, and at her expense. Her body felt hot, her anger growing. She had as little liking for being laughed at as the next person, especially when it was Neil Saxton who was doing the laughing. 'That's why I'm here,' he added before she could say anything. 'I've come to escort you.'

'What?'

'Your friend, Hannah, the interior designer, whose telephone number you gave me,' he explained helpfully. 'She's invited me round for dinner, and she asked me if I wouldn't mind collecting you and driving you there.'

Rue was seething. Half a dozen acid retorts sprang to her lips, furious denials that she had any need of him to do anything for her, but she realised at once that her anger would simply increase his lazy amusement.

'I'm afraid I'm not quite ready yet,' she told him stiffly, taking refuge in the first excuse that sprang to her mind. 'Why don't you go on without me?'

'And have Hannah and her husband think me ungentlemanly?' One dark eyebrow rose.

The breeze caught her hair, tangling it with warm fingers, ruffling strands of it forward so that it brushed against Neil's shoulder. He reached out and touched it, smiling an odd smile.

'You have lovely hair,' he told her quietly, and when she would have jerked away from him he reached out and curled his finger through the loose strands. It was an oddly intimate gesture, one that made Rue's stomach somersault.

As he released the curl that had wound almost lovingly round his finger, he told her softly, 'I don't mind waiting.'

Rue stepped back from him, torn between fury and fear. He had no right to barge into her life like this, to force his unwanted presence on her—and what on earth did Hannah think she was playing at? She would have something to say to her friend when she got her alone.

Knowing there was not a single thing she could do about it, other than refusing to go to the dinner party at all like a sulky child, Rue retreated into the house. The good manners instilled into her by her old-fashioned upbringing would not allow her to deliberately dawdle until the man waiting downstairs for her got so fed up that he left. That wouldn't be fair to Hannah, and no matter how angry she might be with her friend Rue could not bring herself to ruin Hannah's dinner by arriving late.

All that she could do, when she slid into the passenger seat of Neil's car and waited for him to join her, was to say frostily, 'I hope you realise that none of this was my idea.'

CHAPTER FIVE

HANNAH greeted them in a slightly flustered manner, and no wonder, Rue reflected, looking meaningfully at her friend as she told her how surprised she had been to be offered an escort.

'When you told me this was a business dinner, I had no idea that Neil was your potential client.'

Hannah gave her a sweetly vague smile. 'No, well, I don't suppose you would,' she agreed mildly. 'Oh, and I haven't thanked you yet for passing my name on to him. He's invited me to go round to the house as soon as I've got a free afternoon. Apparently he wants me to organise a suite of rooms for his mother. She lives in Brighton, but she comes to visit him several times a year. He was telling me that this is the first proper home he's owned,' she added conversationally as her husband drew Neil out into the garden to show him the progress they were making with their plans to install a swimming pool.

The small Georgian rectory Hannah and her husband had bought several miles outside the local market town had been very dilapidated when they took it over. Now every single one of its rooms was a charming testament to Hannah's skill and home-making qualities.

'It was such short notice that I've only been able to throw together a rather scratch meal,' Hannah apologised as Rue followed her into the kitchen.

'Why go to the bother of having a dinner party at all?' Rue asked her. 'Obviously Neil intends to give you the business.'

'Well, yes, but when he said that he was living on his own and hadn't had time to find a house-keeper yet, I thought how lonely it must be for him. He told me that he hasn't been here long enough to get to know many people, although I must say that I'm rather surprised at you,' she added, arching her eyebrows. 'You never said a word to me about having a new neighbour.'

Rue shrugged and turned her back on her friend so that Hannah couldn't look at her too closely. 'You know how it is for me at this time of the year. The last thing I want at the moment is to be constantly pestered...'

'Pestered?' Hannah interrupted her laughing. 'By a man like Neil? My dear, I know at least twenty women who would give their eye-teeth to have a man as eligible as he is move in next door to them.'

She saw the way her friend's mouth tightened and apologised instantly. 'I'm sorry, Rue. I forget sometimes what a hard time you've had, but all men aren't like your husband, my dear.'

'Aren't they?' Rue asked her bitterly. 'Why exactly do you think Neil Saxton agreed to bring me here tonight, Hannah?'

Hannah looked flustered and turned her attentions to the watercress soup she was ladling out into bowls. 'Oh, I...'

'Not because he's attracted to me, if that's what you're thinking,' Rue told her brutally. 'It's my land he wants, not my body, although I suspect he's quite capable of pretending that there's nothing he wants more than to take me to bed, if he thought that would make me sell the land to him.'

'Oh, Rue, no, I'm sure you're wrong!' Hannah exclaimed in shocked accents. 'He doesn't strike me as that kind of man at all.'

Rue gave her a mocking look and said caustically, 'They're all that kind of man.'

Suppressing a faint sigh, Hannah acknowledged that it was pointless to argue with Rue. She, personally, had found Neil Saxton charming, and, very much in love with her husband though she was, she had been pleasurably aware of Neil's very vibrant maleness.

Poor Rue, she reflected sadly as she allowed her friend to help her carry in the bowls of soup. She had no idea what she was missing. Hannah herself had been so lucky in her marriage, in her husband, in virtually everything in her life, she acknowledged as she went to call the men in from the garden.

Surprisingly, the evening passed very quickly, Rue discovered when the plates had all been cleared and stacked in the dishwasher by Neil and Tom Ford, while she and Hannah prepared the coffee and carried it into the conservatory.

'I'd like to do something like this with mine,' Neil commented, looking approvingly round the lacy Victorian edifice which Hannah had decorated so simply and so attractively. 'Something like this would look much better in my conservatory than the furniture which is already there. Don't you agree, Rue?' he questioned, looking across at her.

Rue gritted her teeth as she caught Hannah's surprised glance, her irritation growing as Neil continued blithely, 'I invited Rue round for dinner last night. I wanted her advice on what I could do to improve the rooms I'm putting on one side for my mother, but she very properly directed me to you.'

Rue could have killed him. She could see the speculation and curiosity brightening Hannah's eyes. Her friend was an incurable romantic and refused to believe that Rue would not be far happier married than she was on her own. Unable to stop herself from scowling Rue put down her coffee-cup.

'I really ought to go,' she said abruptly. 'I have to be up early in the morning. The weather forecast isn't too good. They're predicting thunderstorms within the next couple of days.'

'Oh, Rue, just when you don't want them!' Hannah exclaimed, instantly sympathetic. 'What will you do? Will you be able to get your crop in in time?'

'Yes, I think so,' Rue assured her, 'although the flowers could have done with another two or three days.'

She was unaware of how much her voice revealed, her shoulders hunching slightly as she acknowledged how very hard she was going to have to work.

'What exactly is involved?' Neil questioned sharply, breaking the silence that had fallen. 'Do you employ anyone to help you gather the blossoms?'

'I was going to,' Rue admitted, 'but there isn't time now. I normally ask Mrs Dawson at the post office to find out if any of the local teenagers want to earn some extra pocket money, but by the time

I've got something organised it would be too late.
I was hoping for another week of this good
weather.'

'I'd offer to come and help you,' Hannah told
her, 'but I just can't at the moment.'

Rue shook her head tiredly. 'If I could use your
telephone to ring for a taxi . . .'

Out of the corner of her eye she saw that Neil
was frowning. 'There's no need for that,' he told
her grimly. 'I'm taking you home.'

Rue turned to him, trying to keep her voice and
her eyes cool, desperately conscious of Hannah's
interested concentration on what they were saying.

'You and Hannah will have things you will want
to discuss,' she told him formally.

Over her head, Hannah and Neil exchanged a
mutually understanding look. 'Oh, no,' Hannah
assured her cheerfully. 'We can discuss everything
I need to talk about when I go to see the house.
There isn't really much point in saying anything
until I know exactly what Neil has in mind—and
how much he wants to spend,' she added with a
chuckle.

Knowing that she was defeated, Rue gave in.

It was just gone eleven o'clock, and still very hot
outside. As they said their goodnights, she felt Neil
move close to her side and determinedly moved
away from him. Now that the evening was over,
she suddenly felt desperately tired. Too tired to
reprimand him about the impression he had quite
deliberately given Hannah by telling her they had
spent the previous evening together; so tired that
when the car slid silently out of the drive its com-

fortable soothing motion encouraged her to lean back in her seat and close her eyes.

She fell asleep as quickly and deeply as a child, causing Neil to glance at her in a mixture of compassion and rueful amusement. As she slept, she turned towards him, frowning slightly in her sleep.

When he eventually reached the cottage he parked outside it and watched her silently. After several minutes he reached towards her and unclipped her seat-belt and then, without disturbing her, went round to the passenger door and opened it, bending into the car and lifting her out as easily as though her weight made no impression on him at all.

She woke briefly once, struggling against the mists of sleep which threatened to hold her prisoner, alarm racing through her veins, but the hands that touched her were so knowing and gentle that her fears eased. Theirs was not the touch she remembered with fear and loathing, and under their soothing hold her panic subsided and she drifted back into sleep.

Neil, who had found her keys, unlocked the door, silenced the ecstatic Horatio and carried her upstairs to her bedroom. He paused in his self-appointed task of removing her dress and looked down at her. Such a very tiny, fragile body and such a fiery, indomitable spirit. He touched her face lightly with his fingers. She would be furious with him in the morning.

He eased the dress away from her body and then paused, looking down at her. Her underwear did little to conceal the soft curves of her body. Heat flared in him and was quickly controlled as he eased her gently beneath the duvet.

Irritated with himself, he went downstairs. He couldn't remember a time when he had been so aroused merely by the sight of a woman's body. He had carried her upstairs in all good faith, and self-disgust bit into his composure as he acknowledged how very tempted he had been to reach out and slowly caress those feminine curves.

Back downstairs, he let Horatio out and waited until the dog had ambled round the walled garden and returned to the back door. Having let Horatio in and made sure the locks were secure, he was just about to go round to the front door and slide the keys through the letterbox when instead he pocketed them, a wry smile curling his mouth as he made his way back to his car.

Rue woke up feeling more refreshed than she had felt in a long time. Her body felt lazy and relaxed, sleepy and supine, and somehow oddly different, as though it possessed a secret and sensuous knowledge that was forbidden to her mind. As she stretched out beneath the duvet, she suddenly became aware that she was wearing her bra and briefs.

A frown touched her forehead, and in the pre-dawn light she saw her velvet dress draped carefully over the back of the bedroom chair. A tiny, nig-gling suspicion began to worm its way into her mind. Why had she gone to bed half-dressed? She frowned and tried to remember what had happened.

She had barely touched her wine over dinner. She had been tired, it was true, very tired, in fact. She could remember how sleepy she had felt in the car on the way back. Suddenly she jerked upright in bed and stared fixedly at the window, as dim and very unwanted memories started to surface. One in particular refused to be subdued.

Someone had been touching her, stroking her skin gently, or so it had seemed. She remembered that she had felt panic and that then the panic had gone when she'd realised the hands on her body were not those of her late husband—but they had been a man's hands. She knew that irrevocably.

As she sat there, her mind turning slowly, focusing her disjointed thoughts, she realised that it was Neil that had touched her, Neil who had carried her upstairs and undressed her. A tiny betraying tremor ran through her body like fire.

Outside it was almost light. She had work to do. She had no time to waste on thinking about Neil Saxton. Knowing how hard she was going to have to work, she forced herself to eat some breakfast, switching on the radio so that she could listen to the weather forecast while she ate. It was worse than she had expected.

Storms were being forecast for the early evening. At best it would take her two full days to get the flowers picked and safely stored away inside. Even if she worked right through from dawn until dusk, she would still not be able to harvest them all.

Her shoulders sagged slightly and she immediately stiffened her spine, telling herself fiercely how well off she was in comparison to thousands of other women. All right, so she was now facing a crisis, which could result in her losing almost a whole year's profit if she did not succeed in rescuing her crop, but sitting here worrying about the financial implications of the forecast storm was not going to help.

Outside the air felt thick with heat and oppression. By the time she and Horatio had walked as far as the first field, her thin T-shirt was clinging clammily to her body, and the sun was still barely over the horizon. At least there was no dew, she acknowledged thankfully. To pick the flowers while damp would mean that they would rot before she had a chance of drying them out. She opened the gate into the field and stood there, surveying the task ahead of her, and then she blinked in disbelief as she saw someone moving determinedly towards her.

'Neil,' she said stupidly, 'what are you doing here?'

Like herself, he was dressed in jeans and a T-shirt. Like hers, his jeans were old and faded. Like hers, his T-shirt was shrunken with age, clinging firmly to his body. Her mouth went dry as he moved and she saw the unmistakable ripple of muscle beneath the thin fabric.

'I've brought your keys back,' he told her, watching the colour run up under her skin as she remembered how he had carried her to bed. And then, before she could argue, he added, 'I thought you might be able to do with some help.'

'Help?' She almost stammered the word, as though its meaning was unfamiliar to her, raising bemused eyes to his, as she said painfully, 'From you? But ...'

'I know what you're going to say,' he interrupted her. 'All right, so I don't know the first thing about flowers, but if you tell me where to start and what to do ...'

He saw the look on her face and added roughly,
'This is no time for pride, Rue. Surely an extra pair
of hands, even *my* hands, are better than nothing?
I heard the forecast this morning,' he added, seeing
the doubt and confusion shadow her eyes. 'Independence is all very well, but will you really risk
losing this,' his arms swept a curve over the field
in front of him, 'simply because of the way you
feel about me?'

She wanted to tell him to go, she *ought* to tell
him to go, but somehow the words stuck in her
throat, tears shimmering at the back of her eyes.
Why on earth was he doing this? It would surely
suit his purpose far more if she were to lose her
crop? She couldn't believe he was actually offering
to help her.

Her throat stung with weak, silly tears. It was
almost too much for her to take in that this man,
who had every reason in the world for standing
aside and letting disaster strike her, was actually
reaching out a hand to help her. It confused her,
threw her off guard, made an almost painful happiness flower deep inside her.

'It's time we got started,' Neil warned her.

The sun was already up, the air still with the
threat of thunder. Trying to gather her scattered
wits, Rue told him which rows of flowers needed
to be picked; how to pick them and how to put
them in the wide trugs she had brought down with
her. Trembling a little, she directed him to one row
of flowers as she started working on another.

Her awareness of his presence made her tense and
clumsy, so that for the first half-hour he was almost
outpacing her as they worked, but then gradually

her tension slipped away as the need to work as fast as they possibly could overwhelmed everything else. At eleven o'clock, despite the fact that they had been working without a rest from five, they had cleared barely a third of the rows.

'Time for a break, I think,' Neil announced, straightening up and stretching.

Her own back felt as though it was on fire, but Rue stubbornly refused to move.

'There isn't time,' she told him grittily, 'but if you want a rest, go ahead.'

He came over and took the secateurs and the basket away from her.

'A rest now will give you more energy for later,' he told her firmly. 'We'll go back to the cottage and have something to eat and drink.' And somehow or other, before she could raise any further objection, Rue found that she was firmly but gently being guided away from the field.

They spent barely half an hour in the kitchen drinking the coffee Rue had made and eating the sandwiches Neil had insisted they both needed. Her back had ceased to feel as though it was on fire and about to break in two, and the tension which had made her deny that she needed a rest had eased as well, and with it the headache that had been threatening.

Unwilling to acknowledge that Neil had been right to insist that they had a rest, Rue walked silently at his side as they headed back to the fields.

'There's no need for you to do any more,' she told him abruptly.

'That bad, am I?' he queried ruefully, smiling at her in a way that made her heart suddenly somersault.

Rue shook her head, unwilling to speak in case her voice betrayed her. In point of fact, he had worked so swiftly and efficiently that she herself had been hard put to it to keep pace with him.

Now, despite the fact that there were no clouds in sight, the sky had a brassy cast to it and there was not a breath of air.

'Phew, you can almost feel the thunder in the air, can't you?' Neil commented, tugging off his T-shirt in a movement that made Rue fascinatedly aware of the smooth movement of his muscles. His skin was lightly tanned, the fine, dark hairs covering his chest narrowing down over his stomach.

Rue watched him out of the corner of her eye, wanting to look away and yet somehow unable to do so.

'Come on, back to work,' he told her cheerfully, reaching out and placing a firm hard hand on the nape of her neck.

The effect of his touch was electrifying. She could feel a fine tremor start in the pit of her stomach and spread out to every part of her body. His touch scorched her, branded her, and yet she was unable to pull herself away from it, and in some unspoken way he knew what was happening to her. His hand tensed against the back of her neck and then relaxed, his fingers gently caressing her nape.

Rue felt stifled, threatened, and as much terrified by her own reactions to his touch as she was by the fact that he was touching her. She drew a deep breath and pulled away from him, saying shakily, 'Don't touch me.'

The brooding look he gave her made her stomach melt, and she had to fight to stop herself being drawn towards him. It was the thunder in the air that was having such an odd effect on her, she told herself shakily, as she turned her back on him and walked away from him. Yes, that must be what it was. It was the threat of thunder and the anxiety that were making her behave so oddly.

They worked until one, and this time it was Rue who called a halt. She must have felt like this before, she acknowledged as she straightened her aching back, but if so she couldn't remember it. She felt as though she would never be able to walk upright again.

'Lunch,' she told Neil briefly, barely able to find the energy to speak.

To her anger, he shook his head, and then motioned towards the clouds gathering on the horizon.

'If we stop now, we'll lose half an hour,' he told her grimly, 'and by the way that cloud's moving, we've got three hours at the most before the storm hits us.'

As she looked towards the horizon, Rue realised that what he said was true. A sick feeling of despair twisted her stomach and she looked from the sky to the field in front of them. They had worked hard and cleared well over half of the plants that needed cutting, but as she looked at the work which was still to be done, the lines of colour wavered in front of her eyes. She wasn't going to cry. She couldn't cry, not now, not in front of him.

Gritting her teeth, she bent back over the seemingly never-ending rows of flowers. Alongside her she could hear Neil working. Horatio growled and whined, moving uneasily.

'He doesn't like thunder,' she told Neil as he straightened his back and looked at the dog. 'I found him in a thunderstorm. He'd been abandoned,' she added tersely.

'Mmm. I bet you didn't know what sex he was when you took him home,' Neil responded in a grunt.

Rue felt irrationally hurt, although she knew the jibe was well-deserved. She worked as she had never worked in her life before, and Neil kept pace with her. No, Neil set the pace, she acknowledged tiredly as she saw him move slightly ahead of her and instantly redoubled her own efforts to catch up with him.

During the middle of the afternoon, she felt the sudden drop in temperature and her scalp prickled warningly. The storm wasn't far away now, although the sun still shone brassily. They had three more rows to go and they had just started on the last of them when out of nowhere it started to rain, heavy, cold droplets of moisture, accompanied by growls of thunder and sheet lightning. Then, without any warning at all, the sky opened above them and rain lashed down, beating at the last remaining few flowers they had not picked.

'That's it!' she heard Neil yell out to her above the sound of the storm. 'Quick, let's get this lot inside before they get damaged.'

She wanted to protest that there were still flowers to pick, but she knew Neil was right, and as he bent and gathered up his full trugs she followed suit. She was out of breath and soaking wet by the time she reached the drying shed, but thanks to Neil's foresight the polythene with which they had covered the trugs had kept the flowers dry.

Inside the drying shed, she stared out at the now almost black sky. The small amount of flowers which she hadn't picked would be lost, but at least they had saved the bulk of them. *They* had saved, she acknowledged painfully, realising how very different the situation would be if she had not had Neil's help. She turned to thank him, but the words stuck in her throat.

'I'm soaked,' he told her, 'and so are you. Let's get inside and get dried.'

Nodding tiredly, she headed for the cottage, aware of Neil at her side even though she didn't look at him. The storm showed no signs of abating, rain lashing at the windows.

'We could both do with a hot shower and a strong cup of coffee,' she heard Neil saying behind her. 'Any chance of you being able to do anything with this?'

He held out his T-shirt, and she saw that it was soaking wet.

'I'll put it in the drier,' she answered.

He came to stand beside her and asked quietly, 'What about the rest of your flowers?'

'Mostly autumn flowerers,' she told him tiredly. 'With any luck, they'll survive the storm. They're all properly staked and tied, and if anything's going to damage them it will be the wind and not the rain.'

'Who's going to shower first?' he asked her. Rue was too tired to care. She gave an exhausted shrug.

'I'll tell you what,' he suggested, 'I'll shower first and then I'll make us an omelette or something, while you have yours.'

She knew she ought to tell him that she wanted him to go home, that she didn't want him here in her cottage, but she was too exhausted to even contemplate arguing with him, and so instead she nodded and slumped into one of the kitchen chairs as he headed for the stairs.

Outside, the rain pounded against the stone walls. Wearily she got up and made her way into the sitting-room, striking a match to light the fire that she always kept made up in there. The cottage felt warm enough, but on stormy nights she found that a log fire was somehow comforting. It made her feel secure and safe. Tiredness seemed to have invaded every bone in her body, and her muscles ached. She longed to lie down and go to sleep.

Instead, she acknowledged tiredly, she would have to go upstairs. Neil should have finished in the shower by now.

CHAPTER SIX

WINCING at the pain in her back, Rue climbed the stairs slowly. At the top she stopped and rubbed the small of her back tiredly. From the landing she looked out at the rain-lashed garden below. Her herbs would suffer very little damage from the storm.

In the field beyond the garden, there were long, flowerless green rows where they had picked the flowers. The sight reassured her. Disaster had been avoided, thanks to the almost miraculous intervention of Neil.

The bathroom door opened behind her, but she was too tired to turn round. She felt the steamy heat surround her and then Neil was standing behind her.

The sky had lightened a little now, the thunder only a distant growl. The noise the heavy rain made drumming down on the roof was oddly comforting. It felt good to be here inside her cottage, protected from the elements raging outside.

'Shower's free,' Neil told her, and she turned round to tell him that his T-shirt was still in the dryer and then froze, her mind going stupid with shock.

One of her towels was wrapped around his hips. The silky hair on his chest was damp. Tiny beads of moisture collected on his collarbone and ran down the centre of his chest. Their movement fascinated her; she was unable to drag her gaze away, and she had an odd, compulsive urge to reach out and catch the droplets as they fell.

She saw his chest lift and fall, heard a soft rumble and realised he was talking to her. She lifted her bemused gaze to his face. His eyes had gone so dark that they looked almost as black as his hair, and that, still damp from his shower, curled slightly at the ends. She wanted to reach up and touch it . . . to touch *him*, she recognised on a sudden shuddering wave of self-realisation.

'Rue.' She heard him say her name sharply once, as though in warning, and then when she didn't respond to it he said it a second time in a different tone, softer, and yet with a hint of unmistakable challenge.

And even then she couldn't drag her gaze away from him, from the darkness of his eyes that seemed to burn into her, from the odd paleness of his skin around his mouth as though he were under an almost unbearable burden of tension, and from his mouth itself.

With eyes like a sleepwalker's she focused on it, unable to look away.

And then, shockingly, the spell that had held her immobile was broken as Neil cursed briefly under his breath and took hold of her.

'What is it you want, Rue?' he demanded unsteadily. 'Is it this?'

And then his mouth, the mouth she had stared at and yearned for until her body ached with the need burning inside her, was on her own, kissing her; not as she had ever been kissed before, but with a fierce, unrestrained male need that touched a chord somewhere deep inside her, bringing her quiveringly, singingly, to life.

She moaned helplessly beneath his mouth, oblivious to reality, totally lost in the dream world she had stepped into. She felt the hard pressure of his body against her and reached out despairingly to touch the hot, moist male flesh. She felt him shudder beneath the tentative stroke of her fingertips, and drew in a sharply ragged breath. Her head was swimming, her body drowning in sensation. She had a sharp, imperative need to know what it would be like to feel his body against her own without the sensation-dulling intrusion of her clothes.

Her breasts swelled and ached, sensations she could dimly remember experiencing long, long ago, but never like this ... never with this sharp, almost unbearable pressure that made her cry out in protest and cling to him.

As though the meaning of the inarticulate cry was immediately known to him, Neil lifted his mouth from hers and whispered thickly against her lips, 'Yes! Yes!'

And as she looked up into his eyes she was dazzled by their dark glitter, spinning free of the known world in a place where only the two of them existed.

She felt his hands on her T-shirt, tugging it free of her body while she stood, deaf, dumb and blind to everything bar the need burning inside her. She shivered when cool air touched her spine, and then moaned softly in pleasure and shock as Neil's hands spanned her ribcage.

'You're perfect...perfect...do you know that?' he told her rawly, and her head tipped back

languorously under the pressure of his mouth as he
caressed the smooth line of her jaw, and then her
throat, with tiny, biting kisses that became abruptly
more intense as he reached the swell of her breasts.
His hands cupped her, burning her flesh through
the fine cotton of her bra. His fingers found the
hardening centre of her breast and traced it urgently, as though unable to resist the temptation.
She felt the quickened thud of his heart and her
own pulse mimicked its unsteady beat. He muttered something quick and savage against her body
and she trembled with delight and arousal.

Her breasts, so sensitive to his touch, ached tormentingly as he dragged away the unwanted barrier
of cotton. Against the darkness of his hand, her
skin looked flawlessly pale, milk-white and blue-
veined, her nipples flushed darkly pink. She felt
hot and weak and oddly boneless, as though she
had no ability to move unless he commanded her
to do so. His hand supported her spine, his hair
still damp as he lowered his head towards her breast.

Her whole body pulsed with desire and need...a
need she had experienced before, centuries ago.
Blindingly she suddenly remembered that
need...surely a pale shadow of what she was feeling
now, but a need none the less. Then, too, she had
wanted to give herself, to give and be given...to
love. And then had come the bitter shock of
reality...the knowledge that she was neither loved
nor desired.

She heard Neil moan as his mouth found the
swollen peak of her breast and fastened on it,
bathing it with a moist heat that sent sharply

piercing darts of pleasure hurtling through her body.

But it was too late. The weakness that had stolen away her reason had lifted and she was able to see reality again. Neil didn't want *her*, he wanted her land.

With a tiny sob of anguish, she pushed him away. He released her reluctantly.

'It's no good,' she told him huskily. 'I know why you're doing this. You're just like Julian. You're all the same. You think you can coerce me into selling my land to you...'

The flat, metallic grey of his eyes frightened her, but she wasn't going to let him see it.

'I want you to go. Now...'

'Like this?' he demanded grimly, and she realised that all he was wearing was her towel. Mesmerised, her glance clung to the dark line of hair arrowing down over his belly.

'Rue,' he said softly, 'let me...'

'No,' she interrupted sharply, panicked by her own vulnerability to him. 'You're wasting your time. I'm not as stupid as you seem to think. I might have fallen for that trick once, but I'm not falling for it a second time.'

He looked at her for a long time and then he said quietly, 'Yes. I think you're probably right. Your husband wronged you, Rue, no one could deny that. When I first realised the truth about you, I thought how brave you were, I admired you for it; but now I realise that you're not brave at all. You're a coward... a coward who's hiding behind her bitterness and resentment... who's using the memory of one bad experience to keep the rest of the world at bay.

'All right, so your husband cheated you and hurt you. I'm sorry for that, very sorry, but I'm *not* your husband, Rue. I'm a different man with a different set of feelings.'

'But not a different set of motives,' Rue shot at him. 'You want something from me just as he did, and you don't care what methods you use to get it, just like him.'

He looked at her, and the odd mixture of pity and contempt in his eyes made her want to cry out that he was not to look at her like that.

Without a word he stepped past her and into her spare bedroom, leaving her staring numbly into space.

She was still standing there, her eyes huge with anguish, when he came out, dressed once more but minus his T-shirt.

'In the circumstances, I don't think there's much point in my staying, is there?' he asked her quietly, and even though her mind shrieked triumphantly at her that it had been right and that he had only wanted to deceive and use her, her heart ached with a pain so intense that she had to turn away from him in case he saw it in her eyes.

He stepped past her as though she was unclean, his every movement rigid with dislike. She knew she ought to thank him for what he had done, because, whatever his underlying motives, without his help she would have lost well over half her crop, and that meant all her profit, but the words just wouldn't come.

She didn't go downstairs until she heard him leave the house. She still hadn't had her shower. She was wet and cold, and her teeth were chattering. She went into the sitting-room where she had lit the fire and knelt down in front of it.

Horatio, coming in and finding her crouched there motionless, apart from the tears that ran silently down her face, whined and went up to her.

The warmth of his solid body was comforting, but it wasn't the comfort she wanted, she acknowledged miserably. What she wanted was Neil and that knowledge almost destroyed her. *How* had it happened? *Why* had she let it happen?

All those years ago with Julian she had felt desire, had known and gloried in the intensity of her feminine needs, had joyfully and heedlessly looked forward to her marriage and the pleasures she and Julian would share, because despite her urgings he had refused to make love to her until they were married, and she had secretly been flattered and pleased that he had put his concern for her above his own desire.

How naïve and trusting she had been; but once she had realised the truth, once she had discovered what men really meant when they spoke of love and passion, once she had realised how vulnerable and defenceless her own body could render her, she had made a vow that she would never, never allow herself to be caught in the same trap again. Better never to experience desire, when she knew the pain it could lead to.

Not all men were the same, she had been forced to admit; she had friends who were happy and fulfilled, women who loved and were loved in return, so the fault must lie somewhere within herself. It must be because *she* was unlovable that she drew users and abusers to her... she attracted men who only wanted her for their own gain.

For five, almost six years she had lived by the rules she had laid down for herself. For that length of time she had been safe and content, and then Neil Saxton had forced his way into her life, confusing her with his actions, deliberately and cold-bloodedly setting out to deceive and destroy her... just like Julian.

Time passed, but she had no real awareness of its passage. Darkness fell and Horatio, hungry and alarmed by the unmoving stillness of his mistress, whined pathetically.

The thunder returned, rolling noisily around the hills.

'Imagine it as a giant football being kicked from hilltop to hilltop,' her father had told her as a child. Rue shuddered. She felt icy-cold, stripped of her pride and self-respect, alone in a way she had never felt before. She wanted to close her eyes and go to sleep and stay that way, but Horatio was whining, and the fire had gone out. She had things to do. She was a woman now and not a child. Somehow she must find a way of repairing the damage Neil had done.

Locking the stable door after the horse had bolted, she mocked herself acidly as she got tiredly to her feet, wincing at the onset of pins and needles in her cramped flesh.

She knew of only one way to keep her pain at bay, and that was to work, but right now her body needed sleep, even if her mind did not.

She recognised in some dim, distant way that she probably ought to have something to eat, but there seemed little point. She had no appetite and even less energy. She fed Horatio and let him out. He came back with muddy paws and a wet coat. She rubbed him dry and switched out the lights, making her way reluctantly to bed.

Neil had helped her, yes, but he had exacted a terrible price for that help, a price she was never going to be able to stop paying.

Her heart shuddered and slammed into her ribs as she recognised the truth. She had fallen in love with him. How, she had no idea. Logically it should have been impossible, but when had emotions ever been subject to logic? What frightened her most of all was the knowledge that, had it not been for that saving moment of sanity earlier in the evening, she would willingly, gladly have given herself to him, and would have rejoiced in doing so.

And he would have used her love for him to get what he wanted from her. Just like Julian.

Her love for Julian had been no more than a teenager's infatuation intensified by the death of her father and her need for someone to lean on. The first night of their marriage had been enough to destroy that infatuation: the cruelty of Julian's possession of her—a possession, he had let her know in no uncertain terms, that came only because it trapped her legally into continuing their marriage—plus the realisation that he had never loved her, never desired her, that he had wanted her money and not her—all that had killed her feelings for him completely.

Traitorously, an unwanted thought wormed its way into her mind. Perhaps if she had encouraged Neil to make love to her, she might have discovered that her feelings for *him* would disappear... Angry with herself, she dismissed the thought, recognising it for what it was. Her body ached for him, wanted him so urgently, so painfully that it threatened to overrule the strictures of her mind. And she could not allow that to happen.

She woke up exhausted, her mind drugged to a state of torpor by the nightmares she had endured. To add to her mental misery, her body was stiff, her muscles locked and protesting as she started to move.

She went downstairs in her dressing-gown to let Horatio out and then slumped over the kitchen table, holding a mug of instant coffee...too drained to go to the trouble of making the filter variety she preferred.

The sky was grey and sullen; the previous night's wind had dropped and so had the temperature. Puddles reflected the metallic sheen of the sky. No watering would be necessary today, she reflected grimly. She would have to spend the day in the drying shed, dealing with yesterday's crop, and there would be no Neil to help her.

The air in the kitchen suddenly seemed to choke her and she had to open one of the windows.

Reluctantly she dragged herself upstairs to get showered and dressed. From her window she could see as far as the farmland which Mrs Dacre claimed had been sold. She frowned as she looked at it. What on earth had possessed the builder to buy it? He would have no access to it. She frowned as she remembered how unpleasant and threatening he had been to her. He was the kind of man who was so contemptuous of women, and so very arrogant in his assumption that he could take whatever he wished from life, that even if she had been tempted to sell she suspected she would have refused simply for the pleasure of refusing him.

She grimaced a little to herself as she remembered how he had warned her that he hadn't given up. And now he had bought some other land. She was a little surprised that he hadn't bought the Court instead, and then she remembered that the building was listed and that he was hardly likely to have been granted planning permission.

She was just turning away from the window when she heard the sound of a shotgun being fired. The shots came from Neil's land and she frowned, wondering what he was shooting. Odd parties of youths sometimes spent their weekends shooting over the farmlands after the harvest had been gathered in, their prey rabbits, and during that time of year, early in the morning when the mist still lay on the fields, her Sunday peace would be destroyed by the sound of shots. But it was unusual to hear anyone using a gun at this time of the year.

Tiredly she went downstairs, determined to cast Neil Saxton firmly from her mind . . . and from her heart. Something told her that that was not going to be easy.

Work and more work, that was what she needed, and she certainly had no lack of it, she admitted wryly, as she made herself some fresh coffee and slid bread into the toaster. While she waited for it to toast she went to the back door and opened it, calling Horatio. His morning amble was normally a fairly perfunctory affair. He liked his breakfast too much to linger outside for very long.

She waited to hear the familiar sound of his metal disc clinking against his collar as he came crashing through the undergrowth. A clumsy dog, her Horatio, but a lovable, protective friend.

When she heard nothing she called again. Her toast popped out of the toaster, but she ignored it, a sudden inexplicable sensation of fear crawling down her spine. That shot... Horatio loved to chase rabbits, even though he never caught any. Could Neil...? But no. He would have seen the dog...would have realised... Clumsily she reached for her wellington boots and pulled them on, not stopping to examine the panic that engulfed her, but running unsteadily towards the gate that led into the field.

For once she paid no attention to her flowers, squelching down the muddy path, intent on reaching the stile that led into the home park.

It was *her* fault if anything had happened to Horatio... She shouldn't have let him stray on to someone else's land...but the previous owners had been there so rarely, and Horatio so enjoyed his harmless pursuit of the rabbits that lived in the home park.

She reached the stile and found she was slightly out of breath. She climbed it and from the top surveyed the park, frantically calling Horatio's name. The sound of her voice disturbed some rooks, making them caw noisily as they rose from their untidy nests with flapping wings. Rue ignored them, hurrying in the direction of the stream, which was

Horatio's favourite hunting ground. He had some Labrador in his mongrel ancestry, and enjoyed pretending that he was a water-dog.

The stream skirted through the copse that lay between the home park and the farmland. Rue had seen her first kingfisher there, and, on one never-to-be-forgotten occasion, an otter playing sleekly with the water. The stream had always been a place of magic to her, an emotion left over from her childhood when she had quite happily played on its banks, but today... She remembered that the shots she had heard had come from this direction.

No matter how much she called his name and strained her ears, there was no familiar sound of the heavy, clumsy body panting through the undergrowth.

Almost frantic with fear, she reached the stream and saw at once the paw-marks in the soft mud at the edge of a particularly high piece of banking. She ran up to it and looked down towards the stream.

Horatio was lying on a tiny island of grass and mud, the stream abnormally swollen from the previous night's rain. He whimpered when he saw her and tried to lift his head, yelping suddenly in pain. As he moved, Rue saw the trickle of blood matting his fur on his hind quarters.

She went cold with shock and disbelief. Part of her had been prepared for this, and yet part of her—by far the larger part, she recognised sickly now—had not been able to believe that Neil would do such a thing. That he could hurt *her*... yes, she could understand that... but to hurt Horatio, who virtually worshipped him...to cold-bloodedly shoot her dog...

She raised her hand to her face to push angrily at whatever it was that was obscuring her vision and discovered she was crying. She scrambled down the bank and waded out to Horatio. The dog whined again and thumped his tail.

His flesh was torn where the bullet had hit him, and he was bleeding from the tear. He whined again and tried to stand up, collapsing with a whimper of pain when his leg refused to support him.

It wasn't broken, Rue decided, and as though her presence gave him a surge of strength he managed to stand up and balance himself against her. He couldn't walk home, she acknowledged, hugging him fiercely in her relief that his injuries seemed relatively minor.

He was not a brave dog, and he was shivering now, so glad to have been rescued. She would have to carry him back to the house.

He was a heavy dog, and she was only small. She looked at the steep bank and acknowledged that she couldn't climb up it with him. She would have to walk downstream until she could find an easier way out.

It wasn't easy. Her boots slipped on the moss-covered stones underneath the water, and more than once it swirled in over the top of her wellingtons, soaking her socks and feet. More than once she feared she was going to lose her balance, and more than once she had to stop to rest her arms, but at last the bank shelved down and she was able to stagger out of the stream and on to the footpath.

All she had to do now was to cross the park, and then climb the stile, and then...but one task at a time, one goal at a time.

The stile proved the hardest part, and she wished bitterly that all she had to negotiate was a gate.

The relief of being back on her own land turned her legs weak, but she couldn't stop now. She had to get Horatio back to the house. She had to ring the vet and get him out to see what damage had been done and most of all she had to report Neil Saxton to the police, she thought bitterly.

By the time she had reached the gate from the fields into her own garden, she was so exhausted that it was only instinct and sheer stubborn determination that kept her going. Her arms ached so much, she felt as though the muscles were on fire, as though they were being relentlessly torn from their sockets. Her back threatened to break in two and her legs were trembling so badly that she dared not stop to rest in case they gave way beneath her.

In her arms Horatio whined and whuffled. The blood from his wound had flowed over her arm where the water from the stream had washed it liberally all over her. Once she had lifted her hand to push her hair out of her eyes, and a streak of blood smeared her face.

Totally exhausted, almost blinded by the tears of fear and tension she dared not shed, she realised suddenly that she had almost made it to the back door. The cottage wavered in front of her, somehow dipping and lifting in the most odd way, and then her knees buckled beneath her, and as she cried out in protest a pair of strong arms reached out and lifted her burden from her, while above her head

Hannah's familiar voice exclaimed in horrified accents, 'Rue...my dear! What on earth's happened?'

Hannah? Rue focused on her friend with difficulty and then on the man at her side. The man holding Horatio, soothing him...watching her with such an air of anguished concern that she could not stop herself from saying harshly, 'If you really want to know, why don't you ask him?'

She saw the look Hannah and Neil exchanged and demanded bitterly, 'Go on, ask him. Ask him why he tried to make love to me last night and why he tried to kill poor Horatio...'

'Rue...' She heard the warning note in Neil's voice, but she ignored it.

'I've got to get Horatio to the vet...'

'I'll take him.'

The curt male voice seemed to reach her over a distance. She was conscious of a tremendous sense of weakness and despair, and an equally strong need to fight it.

'So that you can have another go at killing him?' She was shaking now, tears pouring down her face. 'Not much of a shot, are you? Put my dog down... Do you honestly think I'd let you take him anywhere?'

He was standing right in front of her, but in some peculiar way she couldn't focus properly on him, his shape was becoming a dark blur which moved frighteningly.

She heard him saying grimly, 'Hannah, I think you'd better call a doctor...' And then the world faded into blackness, suffocating and engulfing her.

When she came round, she was lying upstairs on her own bed. Hannah was standing beside her, watching her worriedly.

'It's all right,' she told her. 'You fainted. And no wonder, carrying poor Horatio all that way. Neil's taken him to the vet,' she added, seeing the concern darkening Rue's eyes. 'Oh, Rue, you don't honestly believe that *Neil* shot him, do you?' she asked worriedly, dropping to her knees at the side of the bed.

Rue turned her face away from her friend, reading in Hannah's eyes her inability to share her belief, but then Hannah didn't know him as she did...didn't realise how ruthless and cruel he could be.

'I've sent for the doctor,' Hannah told her quietly. 'I think that should be his car now.'

'I don't need a doctor,' Rue told her, struggling to sit up. 'What I need is the telephone so I can report Neil to the police. When I heard those shots this morning...' She drew a ragged breath while Hannah gave her a concerned and disquieted look.

'I'd better go down and let the doctor in.' At the door she hesitated. 'Rue... I think you should talk to Neil. He *can't* have shot Horatio.' She broke off as the front door bell clanged.

'You can believe what you like, Hannah,' Rue told her aggressively, 'but you won't convince me...'

The doorbell clanged again, and with another concerned look at her friend Hannah hurried downstairs.

It was quite some time before she came back with the doctor, and Rue looked at them both suspiciously, wondering what she had told him. Probably that she was off her head, she thought bitterly. It was plain that Hannah was never going to believe that Neil Saxton was responsible for Horatio's wound.

It wasn't Dr Kendrick, whom Rue had known since she was a child, but one of his partners, a brusque Scot with sandy hair and sharp pale blue eyes, and firm fingers that registered her racing pulse and overwrought state while he listened to Hannah's brief explanation of how she and Neil had discovered Rue staggering back to the house carrying Horatio.

'Neil . . . Mr Saxton has taken the dog to the vet. He said he thought it was just a flesh wound, and that Horatio would be all right,' she added for Rue's benefit.

A fit of trembling seized Rue and, for no reason she could think of, tears suddenly started to pour down her face.

'Shock,' she heard the doctor pronounce, his voice fading as he added quietly, 'I think she's going to faint again.'

This time, when she came round, two pairs of eyes were watching her, Hannah's anxious, and the doctor's assessing. She had no right to be lying here like this, Rue thought fretfully; she ought to be on the telephone to the police, reporting Neil's crime.

She heard the doctor say something about 'exhaustion' and opened her mouth to deny it, but a horrid weakness seemed to have invaded her, and when he asked Hannah to fetch a glass of water and handed Rue a tablet, she found that somehow or other she was swallowing it. A very short time after that, or so it seemed, she was floating weightlessly into a warm void where her aches and pains vanished completely.

CHAPTER SEVEN

Rue woke up abruptly to find her room in pitch darkness and the door closed. She normally left it open and the lights on in the hall downstairs, a habit she had fallen into when she first started living alone.

She half stumbled and half fell out of bed, her body a mass of aches, especially her arms. Her mouth felt dry—a legacy of the drug the doctor had given her.

As she went towards the light-switch she heard a familiar whimper, and her eyes, accustoming themselves to the dark now, picked out the shape of Horatio's basket.

Shakily she switched on the light and then crouched down on the floor beside the dog. The wound had been attended to and cleaned, the bare patch of flesh gleaming pinkly against his dark fur. His tail thumped ecstatically on the floor. Rue put her arms round the dog and hugged him, whispering his name.

The bedroom door opened and she froze, hugging the dog protectively towards her as she saw Neil standing there.

From where she was kneeling on the floor, he seemed to tower over her; the dark robe he was wearing revealed a long and very muscular length of leg, instinct telling her that beneath the robe he was naked. She, in contrast, was wearing her underwear, with a nightshirt over the top, and she had a vague memory of Hannah helping her into it, so vague and clouded that she wasn't sure whether it had been reality or a dream.

'I heard you moving about,' Neil told her, as calmly as though there was nothing untoward in him appearing in her bedroom without invitation looking as though he had just got out of bed, his dark hair tousled and untidy. 'I thought I'd better come and reassure you about Horatio. The vet checked him over very thoroughly. Whoever shot him wasn't very accurate. Apart from a flesh wound and shock, he was all right.'

Rue could hardly believe what she was hearing.

'Did you tell the vet that *you* were the one who shot him?' she demanded fiercely. 'Because I certainly intend to... and the police.' She started to shake. 'Get out of here! Get out of my house.' Her hand tightened on Horatio's collar and he whined softly sensing her tension.

'Don't be ridiculous,' Neil interrupted her curtly. 'For goodness' sake, you don't really believe I shot him, do you?'

He broke off as he saw her face. Rue stared back at him resolutely and demanded shakily, 'Didn't you?'

'No, I damn well did *not*.' He was angry now, almost as angry as she was herself, she recognised, and a tiny sliver of doubt touched her like a cold dart of ice. What if she was wrong? But she couldn't be.

'Hannah said you heard shots. What time, can you remember?' he pressed her.

He was trying to trap her, Rue thought. 'It was about nine o'clock. The news was on.'

'For your information, at nine o'clock this morning I had a meeting with my accountants in Cambridge. A fact which I am sure they will be delighted to confirm for you.'

Rue didn't want to believe him. She wanted to protest that a man as rich and powerful as he was could force his accountants to lie to her, but she knew that it wasn't true, just as she knew from the way he was looking at her that she had been wrong.

A horrible hollow feeling inside her chest seemed to cause her heart literally to drop.

'How *dare* you believe that I would wantonly try to hurt or maim *any* animal...and for what purpose? Come down out of the clouds, Rue. Yes I would like to buy this land off you, but I don't want it so badly that I'm prepared to destroy my principles to get it!'

He gave her such a savage look that she quailed beneath it. How had he managed to turn the tables on her and make her feel that she was the one who was at fault...that she...?

She shook herself free of the sensation his anger was arousing inside her and demanded huskily 'Well, someone shot him, or are you going to tell me that I imagined *that* as well?'

'No, he was certainly shot...but whether deliberately or by accident it's hard to know. I understand that the previous owner of the Court rarely visited the place, and that some of the villagers and locals tended to rather make free with the land.'

'You mean that it could have been poachers?' Rue asked.

'Either that, or perhaps a group of teenagers fooling around shooting at rooks and hitting Horatio by accident.'

It was feasible, she knew that, but despite the fact that Horatio had only sustained a minor wound some instinct she could not explain told her that the dog had been shot at deliberately. There had been his terror, for one thing.

'By the way, Hannah was telling me that I'm not the first person to want to buy your land.'

Rue frowned. A glance at her alarm clock when she had got out of bed had showed her that it was half-past one in the morning. She had slept away almost an entire day, and with every minute that passed she felt more alert, in control of herself, but surely the same could not be said for Neil? Surely he must be tired? Too tired, she would have thought, to want to exchange small talk about her land? Unless he was concerned that she might out of spite sell it to the builder.

'No, you're not,' she told him shortly, cross with herself because she felt hurt that he could suspect her of such small-mindedness. If she was to sell to anyone it would be to him; the land had, after all, originally been part of the estate, and it was only fair that if she did he should have the first option to purchase it. Not that she was going to sell. 'There was a builder last year who wanted to buy it. There's been a rumor in the local Press that the land around here might be designated ''white land'' instead of green belt.'

'And so prime land for building development. Especially yours, with its main-road frontage.'

'Well, yes, although that doesn't seem to be important, because he's now bought an acreage behind me from the man who farms what used to be the home farm. Mrs Dacre—that's our old housekeeper—was telling me about it when I went to see her.'

She bent her head over Horatio, stroking the dog's soft fur, and so missed Neil's quick frown.

'He's going to be perfectly all right,' he told her quietly, walking over to the basket. 'I brought him up here because I thought it would reassure you if you woke up.'

A huge lump had formed in her throat at his thoughtfulness. *Why* was he doing it, when he had every reason to dislike her? Surely he must know by now that she wasn't going to sell the land?

'Thank you,' she said huskily, and looked up just in time to see his eyes crinkling with amusement.

'It wasn't so very difficult, after all, was it?' he teased her, and just for a moment she longed to throw all caution aside and to respond naturally and warmly to him, but she couldn't allow herself to do that. She must never forget the cruel lesson loving Julian had taught her...and Neil would hurt her too, if she let him.

Sidestepping his question, she said quietly instead, 'What are you doing here?'

'The doctor said you weren't to be left alone. Hannah volunteered to stay, but since she has a family to look after, I said I'd do it instead.' He looked up at her just in time to catch her expression. 'Rue, for goodness' sake, let the past go, and stop punishing me for another man's sins.'

She was tempted. Oh, how she was tempted, and the knowledge of that temptation, and what lay behind it, panicked her into saying harshly, 'It doesn't make any difference. You...Julian...you're all the same.'

She saw the anger touch his face like lightning, illuminating an expression of such savagery that she shrank from it.

'Well, in that case, you won't find it surprising if I do this, will you?' he told her grittily, and then she was being lifted off her feet and carried over to the bed.

She started to cry out, but the sound was lost as he dropped her down on the bed, and then the weight of him was on top of her, imprisoning her there, his hands pinning down her arms.

Rue tensed, terror surging through her as she remembered her wedding night. They had been married quietly in a register office, which had disappointed her, but Julian had pointed out to her that with her father so recently dead a church wedding might not be seemly.

He had told her that he had rented a cottage from a friend for their honeymoon, and she had pictured something small and intimate in an idyllic setting, but in reality the place he had taken her to had been virtually derelict, and very far from attractive, one of a row of similar cottages, none of which were inhabited, miles away from anywhere outside a grim mining town. The house had been damp and smelled musty. She had later discovered that the house had once belonged to Julian's parents. Tired and disappointed, she had behaved like the rather spoilt nineteen-year-old she had been, protesting that she didn't like the house, until they had quarrelled and Julian had stormed out, taking the car with him.

When he returned in the early hours of the morning, she had been contrite and penitent, eager to make up their quarrel, but Julian had been drunk.

Because of her, he had told her brutally when she had complained . . . because that was the only way he could bring himself to possess her—and he had to possess her to make their marriage legal.

He had spared her nothing then: neither the full reality of his contempt and dislike of her . . . of all those who had the wealth he had not . . . nor his vision of the way their life together would be.

She had fought him at first, until she realised the violence it unleashed in him and the way he enjoyed hurting her.

And now Neil was going to hurt her too.

She closed her eyes and tensed, her body waiting for the pain and humiliation to begin . . . knowing that it must begin and that the only way she could endure it would be to shut herself off from the horror . . . to use her mind to project herself away from it.

And then, unbelievably, she was free, the mattress moving slightly as Neil moved away from her. She was trembling so much that she could hardly move, her heart thudding painfully against the wall of her chest. She opened her eyes and saw that Neil was sitting on the edge of the bed, watching her with an expression she couldn't fathom.

He reached out to touch her and she flinched, unable to stop herself.

From a distance she heard Neil speaking to her, his voice oddly thick and unfamiliar, and as she forced herself to concentrate on his words she heard him say jerkily, 'Rue, I'm sorry. I shouldn't have done that. It was unforgivable. My cursed temper...'

At first she couldn't believe it. He was actually *apologising* to her. Julian had *never* apologised, he had laughed at her fear... had *enjoyed* her fear. Neil, on the other hand, looked white with shock. He lifted his hand from the bed and she saw that it was trembling. She looked into his eyes and saw the same fear and pain in his that she knew was in her own, and from some previously hidden well of compassion she had never guessed existed, her own hand crept out and covered his in a wordless gesture of comfort.

She saw the agony in his eyes darken them to slate-grey as they glittered with a dampness that made her heart turn over in her chest. As she stared wonderingly at him, unable to believe she was responsible for such emotion, he raised her hand to his lips and uncurled her fingers, pressing his mouth against her soft palm.

The gesture, wholly without sexuality though it was, made her body stir like the branches of a young willow tree in a spring breeze.

His lips moved against her skin and she heard him saying roughly, 'Rue. The herb of grace. Your parents named you well.'

And then quick tears stung her own eyes and she said huskily, 'It was as much my fault as yours. I shouldn't have made you so angry. Julian...'

'No,' he interrupted her harshly, dropping her hand, and then when he saw the way her eyes clouded he cupped her face and said more quietly, 'No, Rue. You *did* make me angry, that's true, but anger, no matter how justified, is never any excuse for violence...especially sexual violence. I abhor such cruelty. I always have and I always will. You can't know what it does to my self-respect to realise how close I came to...'

She couldn't let him go on and so she rushed in breathlessly, 'There's no need to feel like that. You didn't hurt me.'

'Hurt you?' She saw his eyes turn almost black. 'Don't you understand even now?'

Her mouth trembled and he seemed unable to stop looking at it. She saw him shudder, felt it in the convulsive movement of his fingers against her skin.

'I didn't want to *hurt* you, Rue. I wanted...oh, hell,' he muttered thickly, unable to drag his gaze away from the softness of her mouth and its innocent provocation.

Rue knew he was going to kiss her, just as she knew that she could quite easily have stopped him, but she felt no compulsion to do so...no compulsion to do anything other than melt against him with an inarticulate sound of pleasure as he brought his mouth down to hers, hesitantly and gently, so that she knew how afraid he was of hurting her, his body rigid against hers, the muscles in his arms corded with strain as he cupped her face and fought to control the need raging through him.

Later Rue wasn't sure how she had known that he wanted her, genuinely wanted her for no other reason than that his body ached for her, but she *had* known it, just as she had known that the torment of her mouth trembling against his, clinging to it, would be almost more than his self-control could stand.

Quite from where she had gained the knowledge that the tip of her tongue tracing the outline of his lips, lingering provocatively on the bottom one and slipping between their parted hardness, would make him groan in protest and then draw her tongue into the heat of his mouth, his control splintering so that she could almost feel the desire running like quicksilver through his veins, she had no idea, but gained it she most definitely had.

As he gently pushed her back on the bed, Neil's mouth touched her temples, her closed eyelids, her jaw, the soft curve of her throat, and finally, when she thought she could stand it no longer, her mouth, drinking from it like a man too long denied such sweetness.

Against her body, she could feel the fierce beat of his heart as though it was her own. She ached for him to strip the clothes from her and make love to her properly. To run his hands over her skin, to shape the soft curve of her hips and the narrow indentation of her waist, to cup the fullness of her breasts and place his mouth against their swollen crests. Where once she had dreaded the mere thought of making love, now she ached to do so. She could feel the hard arousal of Neil's flesh and was maddened by the thin layers of fabric that separated them, and still Neil kissed her, his hands holding her shoulders down against her bed, his body hard on hers, making her moan deep in her throat in pleasure...

A pleasure, though, which was quickly turning to frustration as she opened her eyes and looked into his, willing him to read the need there and to answer it. His own eyes were brilliant with desire, but he made no move to touch her, to push away the intrusive layers of her clothes and caress her aching body as she so longed for him to do.

Her womanhood, dormant for so long, refused to be denied the needs he had unleashed in her, so unfamiliar to her that she had no way of controlling them. His mouth slid from her lips to her jaw, taking hungry, fierce kisses, as though he feared that she might be wrenched away from him at any moment, and yet still he made no move to do anything more than kiss her.

It was more than Rue could stand. She reached up and clamped her fingers on his wrists, urging his hands down towards her breasts.

She felt him tense as she moved against him, and saw the fierce darkening of his eyes. She knew he wanted her as much as she wanted him, and yet when he spoke her name it was in a kind of desperate denial which she did not want to hear, so she turned her head and placed her mouth against his, willing him not to reject her. Tears stung her eyes and her body trembled with pent-up emotion. If he rejected her now she would know that it was all lies, that all his gentleness and kindness had meant nothing, other than that Julian had been right when he had said that she was undesirable, that no man would ever want her for herself.

Without knowing it, she conveyed these thoughts and more to him in the look she gave him, and like a man knowing that he should continue to fight against the tide, even as he knew it was too strong for him, he felt her body move beneath his hands and reality abruptly ceased to matter as he found the opening of her nightshirt and buried his mouth in the scented hollow between her breasts.

In the end it was Rue who helped him to remove her nightshirt and underwear, kneeling on the bed, bathed in moonlight, suddenly proud of her body instead of hating it, knowing instinctively what the curve of her hips, the arch of her spine and the thrust of her breasts were doing to him, and rejoicing in her power over him like a pagan priestess of love.

His own robe was quickly disposed of, her hands deft and exquisitely sure as she untied its belt and slid her palms up over his torso, glorying in the tension of his muscles, the musky scent of arousal that came from his skin, the heat that burst from it as she touched him, stroking and then kneading his flesh with a sensuality she had never dreamed she could know.

And in the end it was she who placed her mouth to his throat, savouring the hot, salt taste of his skin, feeling the tiny pulse jerk and thud as she bit gently while he closed his eyes and shuddered, completely unable to deny his need for her.

Suddenly she felt gloriously free of the past, totally in control of her life, mistress of her own body and of his, and wantonly she let her mouth wander over him, tracing the dark line of hair with teasing kisses until she felt his belly quiver beneath her mouth and he cried out, holding her away from him and looking at her with eyes that glittered with desire-racked hunger.

'No,' he told her hoarsely. 'No, not yet, Rue...it's too soon.'

And as she stared at him, all the confidence and pleasure draining from her, he cursed bitterly, the tight bite of his fingers easing into a caress.

'It *isn't* because I don't want you! Heaven knows, you must know that I do.' And when she continued to stare at him, her eyes frozen lakes of pain, he pulled her towards him and kissed her mouth fiercely, as though willing her to believe him.

He *didn't* want her at all. It had just been pity, pretence...and she had humiliated herself in front of him, shown him... She shuddered and looked past him into the distance, her body suddenly as cold as alabaster.

'Rue, let me explain...'

She focused on him and said tiredly, 'You don't have to. I understand...' And then, like a small child reciting a carefully taught speech, she said formally, 'I'm sorry if I've embarrassed you; I didn't mean to. Too much emotional trauma in one day. There's no need for you to stay. I shall be all right now.'

'Rue——' he began.

She couldn't stand any more. If he stayed much longer, she was going to disintegrate completely.

'Please...' she begged tightly, completely unable to look at him, and as though he guessed what she was having to endure, he picked up his robe and said quietly, 'I'm sorry.'

She closed her eyes until she was sure he was gone. Something told her that no matter what she said he wouldn't leave her here alone, but she drew no comfort from that knowledge, for while he stayed she would be unable to give way to the grief that was tearing her apart.

She loved him, and she had thought he desired her...for wonderful, glorious moments she had thought he wanted her, but it had just been pity, compassion...call it what you would. She had misread the message in his eyes and had caused them both pain and embarrassment.

For both their sakes it would be best if she did not see him again. She because she was not sure she could trust herself not to embarrass them both by revealing her feelings, and Neil... Well, Neil could hardly want to be with her, not now. She had no doubt that, given the chance, he would offer her some face-saving excuse...some tactful explanation of why he had rejected her. Oh, he had tried to pretend that she was wrong, that he did want her, but it had been too late. That hoarse command to her to wait had told its own story.

She sat motionlessly staring into nothing, wondering what it was about *her* that made her precipitate herself headlong into disaster when it came to her personal relationships.

Neil was no Julian, greedy, selfish, uncaring; the only thing they had in common was that neither of them could love her.

As she waited for the pain inside her to subside, Rue acknowledged drearily that it would have been better if she and Neil had never met...if she had never been brought to realise the truth about her feelings for him. Now it was too late to go back and change things. Her body still held an echo of the desire he had aroused within it. If she closed her eyes and ignored reality she could almost conjure up the sensation of his flesh against hers, of his body-heat and scent ... of his touch against her breasts ... of the hot, demanding sensation aroused by the weight of him between her thighs. But she mustn't think about those things. She must obliterate them from her memory and concentrate instead on reality.

She had her home, her business, her friends, and before Neil had erupted into her life she had been content. But now that contentment was gone. The comparison between what her life was and what it could have been if he had shared her feelings was too sharply painful to be borne.

But somehow it would have to be borne. Somehow or other she was going to have to learn to face reality with at least some degree of equanimity.

CHAPTER EIGHT

FOR almost the first time since she had set up in business, Rue felt unable to work; not just because of the physical exhaustion which had weakened her body to the point where all she wanted to do was to simply sit and stare into space nursing a reviving mug of coffee, but also because she had no heart for work. No heart for anything, she acknowledged miserably, bending down to fondle Horatio's ears as the dog whined and thumped his tail on the floor, sensing her misery.

She had brought his basket downstairs into the kitchen, and despite the room's warmth she gave a tiny shiver as she looked at the grey bleakness of the sky outside.

Horatio heard the car before she did, his tail beating frantically, his whine one of obvious pleasure, and before Rue could even think about dashing upstairs to put on something a little more decorous than her nightshirt Neil was at the back door.

It was too late to wish now that she had taken more trouble with her appearance, that she had dressed properly instead of coming downstairs with bare feet and legs, her hair tumbling wildly on to her shoulders, her face untouched by any colour, save that which fluctuated wildly under her skin as she fought to dismiss certain far too vivid memories of the previous night's intimacy.

In spite of herself she felt her heartbeat race into frantic overdrive, a dizzying wave of pleasure engulfing her as she opened the door to him. The only way she could control it was to keep her distance from him as she stepped back to let him into the kitchen.

The first thing that struck her as he walked in was the formality of his clothes. Gone were the faded jeans and worn T-shirt, and in its place was a crisp white shirt, immaculately laundered and starched, and a silver-grey business suit in fine silk and wool. Gold cuff-links flashed dully in the light as he walked over to the basket and bent to stroke Horatio.

'Don't,' Rue cautioned him sharply, causing him to turn round and frown darkly at her. As he straightened up to his full height, she felt vulnerably tiny in her bare feet, uncomfortably conscious of her own near-nudity in comparison with his own formal appearance.

'I'm not going to hurt him,' he told her grimly. 'I thought we'd sorted all that out last night.'

Immediately realising that he had totally misunderstood her, Rue felt obliged to say huskily, 'No, you don't understand. It isn't that——'

His frown deepened and he didn't allow her to finish, cutting in angrily, 'Polite lies, Rue. Somehow I suspected better of you, and anyway it's too late. You've already made it very plain that you're terrified of my touching Horatio. What exactly is it that you think I can do to him right in front of you?' he asked her derisively.

'It isn't that!' she checked him desperately, taking a half dozen steps towards him in her need to correct his misconceptions. He moved at the same time, swinging round towards her, so that she was easily within arm's length of him. Too close for safety, she recognised frantically as his abrupt movement stirred the air between them and she caught the scent of his body, clean, sharp, and yet at the same time very male, conjuring up memories of how last night she had almost been drunk on the wine-taste of his skin and the scent of him.

Her colour fluctuated wildly, her body betraying her agitation. The sudden shuddering breath she drew pushed her breasts against the fine cotton of her nightshirt, and Neil, who had been looking directly into her eyes, suddenly shifted his attention to her body. A tremor shot through her, her insides turned hot and weak.

'It was your suit,' she heard herself saying huskily in a betrayingly strained voice. '*That* was why I didn't want you to touch Horatio. He's moulting, and you'd have been covered in hairs.'

He was listening to her, but he hadn't shifted his concentration from her breasts, and beneath her explanation she could almost hear the panicky clamour of another voice that begged him not to look at her like that, not to expose her vulnerability.

'My suit?'

He was standing so close to her that his breath warmed her skin. His eyes were focusing on hers now, and she felt as though she could drown in their molten gaze. Her body quickened tormentingly.

As she felt the familiar ache tighten her breasts, she glanced down at them, hot colour suffusing her skin as Neil followed her glance and then said thickly, 'You're beautifully sensitive here...'

Her mind went into shock as he reached out and cupped the soft weight of one breast with his hand. 'I couldn't sleep last night for thinking about how you felt and tasted...'

He was lying to her...he had to be. That strained note of desire in his voice was something she had to be imagining. But, because she dared not look up into his eyes and see that he was lying to her, she looked downwards instead, brilliant colour staining her skin as she was left in no doubt of his arousal. 'See what you do to me,' she heard Neil saying somewhere above her head, his voice almost unrecognisable in its fine blend of torment and need. 'Just the thought of touching you has me reacting like a raw teenager. Rue...'

He said her name and somehow or other she was in his arms, whimpering softly beneath her breath at the eagerness which seized her body. One hand tangled in her hair, the other held her waist, as his mouth devoured hers, his tongue fiercely demanding entrance to the moist sweetness beyond her half-parted lips.

In a daze of desire and disbelief she clung to him, her hands clutching at his shoulders until he broke the kiss and muttered something against her mouth, abruptly releasing her. As she stared at him with passion-darkened eyes, her skin chilling as it ached for the heat of his, she thought he was going to leave her, but instead he shrugged impatiently out of his jacket, tugging at his tie and then wrenching open the buttons on his shirt.

'Oh, Rue, don't stand there staring at me like that . . . touch me,' he demanded rawly, taking her back in his arms, pushing her hands inside his shirt and then moaning sharply as she touched him. 'I've been thinking about this all night,' he told her thickly. 'I told myself this morning that I wouldn't . . .'

His hips ground against her as her hands smoothed his skin. He muttered something against her throat, but its meaning was lost as his body spoke for him, the hard pressure of him against her sending all rational thoughts flying from Rue's mind, tiny mewling sounds of pleasure and impatience rising in her throat as she did her best to accommodate the hard thrust of his flesh, moving her body eagerly against his, tiny shivers of delight convulsing through her as he moaned against her skin and his hands found her breasts and kneaded their fullness through the cotton of her nightshirt, increasing the ever-growing ache between her thighs.

His mouth was on hers again, his tongue thrusting urgently into hers, as his body arched powerfully against her.

It didn't need the erotic movement of his tongue and hips to show her what he wanted. She was aware of his need from the tingling tips of her fingers all the way down to her toes.

His tongue touched her lips, caressing them softly, his lips moving tormentingly against hers as he muttered, 'I want you. I want to take you right here and now . . . to fill you with my body, and hear you cry out with pleasure. Is that what you want as well, Rue?' he was asking her urgently, and as though he already knew the answer his hands moved to the hem of her nightshirt, lifting it so that her naked flesh was pressed against him.

Hot excitement licked through her veins, her body responding eagerly to his touch, to the hands that held her hips urging her ever closer to his own aroused flesh.

Desperate for the intimate contact of his flesh against her own, Rue pushed her breasts against his chest, thrilling to the sharp indrawn breath that seized him as he felt the hard points of her nipples rubbing against his skin. His hands slid round to the rounded firmness of her bottom, his hips moving with ever-increasing urgency against her.

His mouth burned her skin, biting into the tender flesh of her throat. Wild with the need he was generating inside her, a need that far outstripped any thing she had ever experienced for Julian, she barely heard the metallic rasp of his zip, nor realised properly the purpose behind his movement as he turned her round and half carried and half propelled her back against the closed door.

The sudden sensation of the hardness of his bare thighs against her, the fine hair that grew there rubbing sensuously against her own far more delicate and tender skin made her go wild with need, moaning softly beneath her breath as her hips mimicked the fierce thrust of his, and his hand moved round to touch her so intimately that she had no defences against the sensations he was arousing inside her.

'You're so soft and moist,' she heard him mutter shockingly against her ear. 'So feminine and tempting. Have you any idea how much I ache to be inside you, Rue?' And then, without waiting for her to answer, he added tormentingly, 'Shall I show you? Shall I show you just what you do to me?'

And then it wasn't just his fingers that were moving arousingly against her, and the need to have him inside her overwhelmed every other consideration and she moved eagerly and enticingly against him, wanting to feel the male strength of him filling the empty ache inside her. She felt his hands on her hips and shuddered mindlessly, anticipating the pleasure she would feel.

In the distance the church bells rang, and then abruptly, so abruptly that she could hardly believe it was happening, Neil released her.

Her eyes opened in pained disbelief to see him standing several feet away with his back to her. She heard him tug up the zipper on his suit, and over his shoulder he said tersely to her, 'I can't stay. I've got to be in London for one.'

As he saw the look of shocked rejection in her eyes, he swore savagely and came back to her.

'Oh, Rue, don't look at me like that . . .'

Pride made her pull away from him, but he wouldn't let her go, holding her against the hardness of his body.

'No, just let me hold you for a minute,' he muttered against her hair. 'You have the most disastrous effect on me, I hope you know that. I came here this morning just to see how Horatio was, and to tell you that I'd be away for a few days, that's all.'

So it was all her fault, was it? She was the one who had deliberately and wantonly tempted him . . . was that what he was trying to tell her?

Her whole body went cold and she pushed him away.

'I'm sorry if I delayed you,' she told him sharply, turning away from him, and then, summoning all her courage and her pride, she turned back to him and said coldly, 'If you're so desperate for a woman that the mere sight of one is enough to arouse you, then perhaps you'd better not come here again. I don't want you in my life, Neil,' she lied, forcing herself to look directly into his eyes, praying that he wouldn't guess at the betraying truth that her lies concealed. That she was so desperately in love with him that she was in grave danger of humiliating herself completely.

'That wasn't the impression I got five minutes ago,' he told her tautly.

For a moment she was lost for words, and then she said huskily, shrugging her shoulders as negligently as she could, 'You're a very experienced and powerful lover...naturally you aroused me sexually.'

'And that's all there was to it, is that what you're trying to tell me?' he demanded grimly.

She had gone too far to back down now. If she did, he might start questioning why she had felt the need to lie and protect herself in the first place.

'Yes,' she lied bleakly. 'What else could it be?'

She thought for one moment that he was actually going to take hold of her, but he seemed to think better of it, because he stepped back from her and finished fastening his tie, and then said curtly, 'There isn't time to finish discussing this right now, but don't think I'm letting it go here, Rue, because I'm not.'

And then he opened the door and walked through it, leaving Rue feeling so mentally and physically drained that she simply could not move.

It was almost half an hour before the full import of what he had said sank in, and when it did she got up and walked unsteadily towards the window, staring in the direction of the Court. It frightened her that she should feel so abandoned and lost simply because he was going away for a few days.

Why was he going to London? What would he do there? Who would he see? Women far more accommodating and sophisticated than she was... women who would be only too glad to take what he was offering and... With a tiny moan of pain, she turned away from the window, glad of the interruption when her telephone rang.

To her surprise it was her solicitor, and the news he had for her surprised her even more. It appeared that he had received another approach from the builder's solicitors, repeating his offer to buy the cottage and its land.

Immediately Rue told him to tell the builder that he was wasting his time and that there was no way she was going to sell.

That night she didn't sleep well, her dreams haunted by images of Neil. She woke up aching with longing for him, unbearably tempted to take what he was offering her and give in to the tormented urgings of her own body, even while her heart begged her to reconsider, reminding her that she wanted much much more from Neil than sexual gratification...that she would never be content with a brief, meaningless affair, which she suspected would cause her more pain in the long run than if she stood firm now and refused to see him again.

And yet, even as this acknowledgement formed, she ached to see him again. To hear his voice...to be with him... She shuddered, acknowledging the power of her love for him, and its potential destructive effect on her life.

She might have thought she had known loneliness before, but she hadn't, Rue acknowledged as three days passed without her seeing or hearing anything of Neil and she had to face the unpalatable knowledge that it was too late now to try and exclude him from her life. Her love for him had grown so unexpectedly, so quickly, that to tear its roots out of her heart was going to be an impossible task.

Wisdom preached that, for her own peace of mind, once he did come back she should see as little of him as possible, and yet every time she remembered the hunger she had seen in his eyes, the need she had felt in his body, wisdom was drowned beneath the demanding voice of her love.

She told herself that it was just sex that he wanted from her, that she was a convenient body—a safely convenient body, an inward voice of cynicism told her, a woman whose age must mean that she was unlikely to have the same foolishly romantic illusions a younger girl might cherish. And yet he had been so tender to her...so kind.

As he would to anyone who aroused his compassion. Compassion and desire, a potentially explosive mixture, but nothing like as dangerous to him as it was to her.

He didn't love her. If he had done, surely he would have told her so, would have spoken of loving her, not wanting her. She had so little experience of the male sex... too little knowledge of their emotional make-up.

Horatio's wound healed; the grey clouds lifted and the sun came out again; her work kept her busy and time should have disappeared like mist in the hot morning sun, but it didn't.

The nights were the worst. Nights when she unrepentantly lay awake remembering how it had felt when Neil touched her. Nights when she deliberately forsook the panacea of sleep in favour of the torment of fevered imaginings of how it could have been if...

And when she lay in bed thinking of Neil so intimately, her body ached for him.

He had been away three days when Hannah came round, cheerfully announcing that she and her family were going away on holiday.

'A friend of a friend has a villa in Spain and they've asked me to revamp the interior.' She looked at her friend's wan face and said shrewdly, 'I suppose there's no point in asking you to come with us.'

Quickly Rue shook her head, and then, conscious of her friend's thoughtful look, said defensively, 'How can I? I'm far too busy for one thing, and for another there's Horatio.'

'Wouldn't Neil look after him for you?' Hannah asked her.

'He's away at the moment,' Rue told her, deliberately turning her head away so that Hannah couldn't guess how much just talking about him affected her.

'Away? Oh, you mean that trip to London,' Hannah answered carelessly. 'No, he's back. He got back last night, or so he told me this morning. He telephoned and asked me to go round so that we could go through the rooms he's putting on one side for his mother. They're lovely,' she added enthusiastically. 'A bedroom and sitting-room plus bathroom on the first floor, overlooking the side of the house. They're over the library, I think. Do you remember them?'

'Yes,' Rue told her shortly. The rooms her friend was referring to had once been her own, but she didn't want to say so. She didn't want to say anything which would encourage Hannah to linger, because she wanted ... no, *needed* to be alone with the pain that was threatening to destroy her.

Neil was back, *had* been back for almost a full day, and had made no attempt to get in touch with her.

It made no difference that she herself had told him to stay away ... her eyes felt sore and gritty and she had a horrible feeling that she was about to cry.

'Most of the work he wants done is simple enough. The rooms are so lovely that there shouldn't be any problem sorting something out. I'm going back home to outline a couple of schemes now so that I can get Neil's approval and put things in hand before we leave for Spain.' She eyed Rue thoughtfully and then told her firmly, 'You're getting too thin, Rue. There's almost nothing of you apart from your chest,' she added teasingly, eyeing her friend's body with rueful envy. 'How is it that when I lose weight, I immediately become flat-chested?' she demanded wryly. 'Whereas when *you* lose it, you immediately begin to look fragile and haunted, all high cheekbones and delicate wrists, and not one single centimetre do you lose off your bust.'

'Genes, I suppose,' Rue offered her absently. It was true that she had lost weight. Food seemed to have lost its appeal completely, and twice since Neil had left she had stopped work in the evening and discovered she had gone all day without eating a single thing.

Hannah stayed a few more minutes, chatting about her proposed trip to Spain. Despite the fact that she had wanted to be alone, once she had gone Rue found the house almost disturbingly empty.

What was it that Neil had done to her that made her find her once-prized privacy something which now made her feel acutely lonely?

She made herself a cup of coffee and called to Horatio. There was still work to be done: the watering, and all the flowers she and Neil had picked, which were now being carefully dried, needed turning and checking.

The very thought made her back ache, and she couldn't help remembering how quickly the time had passed when she had had Neil to help her. How having him there working beside her had encouraged her to work that little bit harder. How, on those odd occasions when he had raised his head to smile at her, her aching back had suddenly been forgotten.

She worked until gone ten, all the time her ears straining for the ring of the telephone, the sound of the car which would herald Neil's arrival, but everything remained quiet. Too quiet, she acknowledged with a tiny shiver as she walked back to the house, Horatio at her heels.

She knew she ought to have something to eat, but she felt too listless, too drained to be bothered. A hot bath and a milky drink, that was all she really wanted.

Lies, an inward voice taunted. You want Neil. And it was all too painfully true, but it seemed that he must have taken her words at face value. Because he didn't rush to see her the minute he got home? she scorned herself. Why should he? She had no importance in his life. She sighed faintly.

She knew even as she went to bed that she wouldn't sleep, couldn't sleep, and, dangerously, she wondered what would happen if she got dressed again and went to see Neil. The worst he could do would be to ask her to leave . . . to tell her that he had no interest in her, sexual or otherwise. How easy it would be to give in to the temptation, but she mustn't. What had happened to her pride? Her self-respect?

It was a long time before she fell asleep, and then Horatio, who was still sleeping in a basket in her room, got up and whined, his doggy ears catching something that couldn't reach those of the woman asleep on the bed.

He looked at her and whined again, and then got out of his basket and padded downstairs, sensing an intruder somewhere outside in the darkness of the night.

It was his barks that woke Rue, sharp, fierce barks that warned of danger, and at first, still muddled by sleep, she thought that Neil must have come round after all, and she sat up, her face wreathed in smiles, her heart thudding frantically, wishing she had thought to wear something a little more exciting than her old nightshirt, trembling with anticipation and pleasure as she waited for him to knock on the door.

Only there was no knock, and Horatio's barks were growing steadily more frantic, punctuated by deep growls that rumbled in his throat.

Calling to him, Rue got up and hurried downstairs, switching on the lights. Sometimes a fox or a badger disturbed his sleep and he barked like this, resenting their infringement on what he saw as his territory. He was standing by the back door, his hair on edge, the growls becoming more and more menacing by the time Rue got down to the kitchen.

She tried to quieten him, telling him that there was no one there, but he refused to heed her, scratching at the door and whining to be let out.

Knowing that he wouldn't quieten until she had done so, she gave in, telling him firmly as she opened the door that there was nothing there. To reaffirm it, she went out with him, shivering a little as the cool night air struck her skin. She hadn't bothered to pull on a robe, and all thought of going back into the house to get one was shocked from her as she walked to the end of the yard and then stopped, arrested by an ominous crackling sound and the smell of something burning.

Instinctively she started to run towards the sound, rounding the corner just in time to see the flames licking greedily at the window on the stable...right next door to the drying shed where she had put the newly cut flowers to dry and where she had thankfully placed nearly all her spare stock, only that week, cleaning out the shelves in the stable ready for the new season's flowers.

Without stopping to think, she raced to the drying shed, flinging open the door and tearing inside, grabbing the nets that held the drying flowers, staggering outside with her arms full and hurrying to put them in the relative safety of the yard.

The thought that she herself might be in danger never even occurred to her. All she wanted to do was to save her stock, and while she worked she wondered frantically how on earth the fire had started. She was always so careful, so very careful...

A small explosion from the stable made her tense fearfully, and she staggered outside to see flames leaping from the loft window.

The fire was spreading quickly; soon it would reach the drying shed. Appalled, she realised the danger that she was in . . . and all that she stood to lose. Not just her business, but her home as well if the flames should spread, and potentially her life, and yet still she stood there, completely unable to move, mesmerised by the lethal tongue of red and yellow fire, ignoring the heat that scorched her skin, and the ominous crackling sound of dry roof-timbers being eaten away by the furious flames, unable to do anything but stand there and watch her whole world being destroyed. She saw the flames burst out through the loft door and burning timbers crash down on the drying shed. She heard in the distance the sound of a fire engine, and just for a moment her head turned towards it, but the flames captured her again. Dry-mouthed, she watched them devour everything she had worked for, while the fire engine raced ever nearer.

She was almost surrounded by a circle of flame when the Daimler screeched to a halt in her yard, its driver wrenching himself out and across the distance that separated them, snatching her off the ground just as a heavy roof-timber burned through and crashed down to the ground, hitting the spot where she had been standing.

'You crazy fool!' Neil told her roughly. 'What the *hell* do you think you're doing? Don't you realise the danger?'

Danger...? Oh, yes, she knew all about that. Her eyes widened and darkened, her gaze fastening on him in shocked panic as she tried to claw her way free. This man was danger...danger and torment and almost unbearable pleasure all rolled into one.

As desperately as she fought him, he refused to let her go, wrapping his arms tightly round her so that she couldn't move hers, swinging her up and carrying her past the helmeted uniformed men who suddenly seemed to be everywhere.

Neil stopped in front of one of them, and Rue heard him saying tersely, 'I don't think there's much you can do to save the outbuildings.'

'No, probably not. How many people are there in the house?'

'Just one. She's here with me. I'm taking her home with me now.'

And then he swung her round in his arms and carried her towards his parked car. Just before he bundled her into the passenger seat, Rue begged hoarsely, 'Horatio.'

'In the back of the car,' Neil told her harshly. 'He seems to have a damn sight more sense than his mistress. What in hell's name were you doing standing there like that? Don't you *realise* you could have been *burned to death*?'

His words brought home the reality of her danger to her in a way that the flames had not. She shuddered and then sagged, sick with shock and reaction, shivering with cold, hugging her arms around her body, and realising abruptly what she was wearing.

'I can't go like this. I need something to wear.'

'You're not going inside that house. Not until the fire brigade announces that it's safe,' he told her curtly, starting the engine. 'For goodness' sake, Rue, what were you doing? You hadn't even alerted them, had you? If I hadn't seen the flames and rung them . . .'

'You rang them . . .?'

'Yes. I'd gone out for a walk . . .'

'At two o'clock in the morning?'

A violent spasm of shaking seized her, and she closed her eyes, unable to pursue her questions. She felt sick with the realisation of the danger she had been in. A danger which Neil had rescued her from . . . only to carry her into an even greater danger. She could be burned just as traumatically and fatally by the flames of her love for him as she could have been by those devouring her home. And who would save her from those?

CHAPTER NINE

As NEIL drove her towards the Court, she had a confused impression of the countryside flashing by. Hedgerows, a darker shade of grey than the pale grey of the fields, all of this silvered by the moonlight. The car tyres squealed protestingly as he turned sharply into the drive. Rue swayed sickly in her seat, wanting to tell him to slow down, but almost afraid to say anything at all to him as she looked at his face and saw the tension and anger in it. She saw the outline of the Court ahead of them at the end of the drive, familiar and yet in some ways unfamiliar to her.

Neil stopped the car and unfastened his seat-belt with jerky, uncoordinated movements. Before she could even reach for hers he was round at her side of the car, opening the door and reaching inside to do it for her, lifting her unceremoniously into his arms.

'I can walk,' she protested, but the words were muffled against his chest, drowned out by the fierce drum of his heartbeat.

Why was he so furiously angry with her? Because she had disturbed his walk? she wondered in confusion. Because he was having to help her out yet again, or because he was being forced into an intimacy with her that he didn't want?

She realised with a small shock that the front door to the Court was standing wide open.

'When I saw the flames, I came back here to telephone you. It was only then that I thought you might be stupid enough to try to tackle the blaze by yourself.'

He shouldered his way into the hall and switched on the lights. Immediately the familiar contours of the room sprang into view in front of Rue's bemused eyes.

'When you didn't answer the telephone, I thought...' Rue felt the shudder that went through him, convulsing his muscles, and making the hand that held on to her tighten almost painfully into her flesh.

'For heaven's sake, Rue!' he demanded abruptly. 'What the hell were you doing out there working at that time of night?'

A vein throbbed in his temple, and his skin, when she looked at it, was oddly flushed. A warm feeling of tenderness and compassion melted her bones.

'I wasn't,' she told him huskily. 'Working, I mean. Horatio woke me up. He was scratching at the door and barking. I thought there must be a badger out there, or a fox. He wouldn't be quiet, so in the end I had to let him out and I went out with him. That's when I heard the flames and smelt the smoke.'

'You were in the house all the time.' He put her down on her feet abruptly, and glared at her. 'Then why in hell's name didn't you stay there?' he demanded. 'What on earth possessed you to go rushing off down there? Didn't you realise the danger you were putting yourself in?'

'I never thought about it,' she told him honestly. She felt peculiarly shaky now that she was standing on her own two feet. 'All I could think about was the flowers, the ones we picked before the storm. I had to get them out.'

'You're joking,' she heard Neil saying tiredly. 'Do you honestly mean to tell me that you risked your life and my sanity to save a handful of flowers?'

His vein was pulsing even harder now, his eyes almost black with fury, but Rue was angry herself now; too angry to care what she was risking or inviting as she lashed back at him.

'A handful of flowers? That's all they might be to you, Neil, but to me they are my living. I couldn't let them be destroyed, not after all the hard work we'd put into saving them. There was almost a whole year's profit in that drying shed. I had to get them out.'

'A whole year's profit.' He was breathing heavily now, glaring at her, making her feel rather like a vulnerable and very new matador faced by an extremely dangerous and maddened bull. She circled him warily, without taking her eyes off his face. 'And just exactly how much is a whole year's profit?' he demanded thickly.

Her anger had died away as quickly as it had arisen, and she was too nervous to lie to him.

'Somewhere about five or six thousand pounds,' she stammered helplessly, hardly daring to look at him as she saw the rage engulf his features.

'Five or six thousand pounds?' he gritted, almost spitting the words at her. 'You risked your life for five or six thousand pounds? Come here.' He practically dragged her into the study and thrust her down into a chair. 'Let me give you a lesson in economics,' he told her. 'If you invested the money I offered you for the land, it would bring you an

annual income far in excess of five or six thousand
pounds.'

Rue knew that it was true. She had no defence
against either his argument or the look that he gave
her. Right from the start she had known that the
money both he and the builder had offered her for
her land would enable her to live in comparative
comfort and without the hard work she was now
obliged to do; but to simply give up after everything that she had done, to put aside all the effort
she had put into making the small business a
success, had seemed to Rue in a way to be turning
her back on everything she had learned from her
disastrous marriage to Julian. It would have been
as though in some way she was reverting to the
spoiled, thoughtless girl she had once been.

She looked at Neil, almost without seeing him,
unaware of the emotions reflected in the sombreness
of her gaze.

'Why?' he demanded thickly. 'Why the hell
punish yourself like that?'

He reached out towards her and took hold of her
hand, grasping her wrist and turning her hand first
palm upwards and then nails upwards, making her
look at them.

'Think what you're doing to yourself, Rue. For
how many more years can you push yourself the
way you're doing now, working single-handedly
almost every hour in the day—and for what?'

'For something far more important than mere
money,' she told him, suddenly finding her voice
again. 'For self-respect, Neil. For the right to prove
to myself that I can be both independent and selfsufficient.'

'And that's very important to you, isn't it?' he asked her cynically. 'Has no one ever told you that no man, nor any woman for that matter, is an island, Rue?'

Of course they had, many, many times, she remembered—when warning her of the isolation she was turning her life into.

'All right, so you were once hurt and badly, but surely that doesn't mean you have to turn your back on the rest of the human race for ever?'

'I haven't,' she told him, shivering a little beneath the force of his words.

'Oh, yes, you have, Rue,' he argued with her. 'You've built a wall between yourself and the rest of humanity. You've told yourself that you don't need anyone or anything, and you're determined not to let anyone behind that barrier you've created to protect yourself.'

'Stop psychoanalysing me, Neil,' she interrupted him sharply. 'Just because my life doesn't fall into the normal pattern for a woman of my age, just because I don't have a husband and two point four children, that doesn't mean that there's anything wrong with me.'

'No, *that* doesn't,' he agreed sardonically, and the colour rushed up under her skin at the way he was looking at her.

Foolishly, recklessly, heedlessly, she ignored the warning signal hammering from her brain and said desperately, 'What exactly are you talking about, Neil?'

'I'm talking about the way you make me feel, and then back off from me,' he told her curtly. 'I'm talking about the fact that you let me get so close and then no closer. I'm talking about the fact that you wilfully and crazily risked your own life rather than ask for help. Doesn't *that* tell you anything about yourself, Rue?'

She was quite proud of the steadiness of her voice when she answered him calmly, 'Only that I like my independence, and I already knew that.'

'You like your independence,' he mimicked her almost savagely, half reaching out to her as though he meant to take hold of her and then wrenching himself away, pushing impatient fingers into his hair and turning to look at her, his face tight with anger and tiredness. 'This isn't getting either of us anywhere,' he said grimly. 'I think we'd both better try to get some sleep for what's left of the night.'

Rue glanced involuntarily towards the window. Dawn was already beginning to lighten the sky. A tremor shook her as she realised that, since arriving at the Court, she had hardly given her own home a thought. As though he read her mind, Neil said quietly, 'As soon as the fire service have anything to tell us, they'll be in touch. I've given them my number here.'

Part of her told her that she ought to object to him taking charge in such a high-handed fashion, and yet part of her, the larger part, she recognised wearily, was only too relieved to have him do so. It had been a long time since she had had someone to lean on. Rue could deceive the rest of the world, but she couldn't deceive herself. There was something within her, some flaw in her character perhaps, that had made her long to admit how willing she was for him to shoulder her problems, if only momentarily.

'There's no need to come upstairs with me,' she said instead, 'if you'd just tell me which room I'm to sleep in.'

He shrugged his shoulders. 'You can take your pick, they're all furnished. I bought the house with its contents.'

'Where are you sleeping?' she asked him quickly, and then her face glazed with hot colour as she saw the amusement leap immediately to life in his eyes.

'At last!' he said teasingly. 'Although I'm not sure if there's enough left of either the night or my energy to do full justice to your invitation.'

Rue didn't know which was the greater, her fury or her embarrassment. He knew quite well that she had not asked which room was his because she wanted to share it with him; far from it. Mastering her anger as best she could, she said coldly, 'If that was supposed to be a joke, I consider it to be in very poor taste.'

Immediately she wished she hadn't been so rash as he came towards her and said smoothly, 'Who's joking? I've been wanting to share my bed with you from the first moment I set eyes on you.' His voice suddenly seemed far too close to the sensual purr of a hunting animal. It made tiny hairs at the nape of her neck stand up on end, and her skin tightened with tension.

She fought desperately against the effect he was having on her and said shakily, 'If I'm supposed to find that admission flattering, I've got news for you.'

'Don't say it,' he broke in, taunting her. 'You'd only be perjuring yourself.'

As the hot, indignant words of denial leaped to her tongue, he added smoothly, 'Your body's giving you away, Rue, and body language speaks far louder than any amount of words.'

She realised too late that what he said was true. Her nightshirt, plain serviceable cotton though it was, did very little to conceal her awareness of him as a man.

'I'm tired. I'm going to bed,' she told him tersely, turning away from him and towards the door.

She was half-way there before she remembered that he still hadn't told her which was his room, and as she hesitated he seemed to read her mind, because he said softly, 'Why don't I just let you find out for yourself which one is mine?'

She lost her temper then, her self-control already frayed not just by his presence but by the after-shock of the fire, and she turned on him and said fiercely, 'The only reason I'd want to know which room is yours, Neil, is that so I can avoid going within half a mile of it.'

She saw from his face that she had angered him, and, while the atmosphere between them tensed to the point of danger, she knew that it was too late to recall her hasty words.

'That wasn't how you felt the other morning,' he reminded her. 'You'd have been only too willing for me to take you where we stood.'

Much as Rue longed to fling an icy retort at him, there was nothing that she could say, no defence she could make. That knowledge shone from her eyes as she turned to give him one last look, and unaware of what she was betraying to him, she saw his own eyes darken a little, and the anger ease out of them as he took a half-step towards her. But she had had enough trauma for one night, and before he could come within arm's reach of her she was out of the room and half-way across the hall.

She deliberately avoided the room which had once been hers, knowing that Neil intended to use it for his mother, and instead chose one of the other bedrooms, opening almost the first door she came to. Having reassured herself that it was unoccupied, she went over to close the curtains and then walked into the en-suite bathroom. It was only as she did so, and saw the door in the opposite wall of the bathroom, that she remembered that this was one of the rooms that shared a bathroom with its neighbour. Not that it mattered; after all, there was only Neil and herself in the house, and he was almost bound to be using the master bedroom, which she knew was down at the far end of the corridor.

She bathed quickly, letting the hot water clean her skin and soothe her tense muscles. The thought of putting her grubby nightshirt back on was not a particularly pleasant one, but caution insisted that she did so. In the morning she would have to ask Neil to drive her over to her house and bring some clothes back for her, much as she hated the thought of being further indebted to him. And then, as she dried herself and pulled on her nightshirt over her head, it suddenly struck her that in the morning she might not have a home.

She had just crawled under the blankets and turned off the light when she heard a brief tap on her bedroom door. Before she could say anything, it opened and Neil came in, carrying a glass of water.

'I've brought you a sleeping tablet,' he told her briefly, putting the glass of water down beside the bed. 'No arguments,' he insisted, when she opened her mouth to tell him she didn't want it. 'I need to get some sleep tonight, even if you don't. I'm still feeling jet-lagged.'

'Jet-lagged?' Her eyebrows rose. 'This is the first time I've heard of anyone suffering from jet-lag after a trip to London.'

'I agree,' he told her grimly, quite obviously disliking her sarcasm, 'but as it happens the jet-lag I'm talking about was incurred on a flight back across the Atlantic from New York.'

Numbly Rue swallowed the tablet and took several sips of water.

'I had a business meeting there,' he told her, almost savagely. 'In fact, I should still be there.' He was looking at her almost as though he disliked her, Rue realised on a sudden shock of pain. 'Aren't you going to ask me why I came back,' he demanded rawly, 'putting my system through hell, not to mention those of the executives that I took with me? They weren't too pleased about a round trip to New York and back, which meant almost twenty-four hours in the air. You see,' he added almost conversationally, 'I had this odd idea that you might be missing me, that you might be eagerly waiting for me to come back so that we could pick up where we left off the other morning, instead of which...' he went on, his voice grating harshly against her sensitive ears, 'I find you on the point of getting yourself burnt alive.'

Rue winced at the picture his words drew.

'But you don't want me, do you, Rue? It was all just a game.'

A game? If only he knew—but he couldn't know. She mustn't let him know. Tiredly she told him, 'If

I wanted you, I'd be sleeping in your room,
wouldn't I, instead of one as far away from yours
as I could make it?'

He gave her an odd look then and seemed about
to say something, but at that moment Horatio came
wandering into the room, demanding attention not
from her, Rue recognised, but from Neil, to whom
he suddenly seemed to have attached himself. Neil
saw her look of surprise and said derisively, 'Unlike
his mistress, this dog seems to know who his real
friends are. Goodnight, Rue,' he added. 'I won't
wish you sweet dreams.'

After he had gone, her mind throbbed with a
hundred unanswered questions. Why was he im-
plying that he had rushed back from New York just
to be with her, when they both knew that it couldn't
possibly be true? Why was he pretending that his
desire for her was so strong that it intruded into his
business life—or did he think that she was silly
enough and vain enough to believe what he was
saying to her? Did he think that he could flatter
her into his bed? Didn't he realise that he had no
need to flatter or beguile her, that he simply had
to touch her, to look at her? Her thoughts grew
cloudy as the sleeping tablet took effect, her eyelids
suddenly so heavy that she had to close her eyes.

Rue opened her eyes slowly and reluctantly,
stretching luxuriously as she did so, conscious of
having slept deeply and very well. As she looked
round the room for a clock, vague, unsettling
memories of what must have been dreams made
her forehead pucker in a small frown. She had
dreamed that the fire was about to engulf her, and
her terror had made her scream out sharply. In her
dream, strong arms had lifted her out of the way

of danger, cradling her against a hard male body, holding her safe, comforting her. As she sat up in the large double bed, she saw a neat pile of her clothes waiting for her in a chair.

Neil must have been over to the house and brought them for her. She drew back the covers to get out of bed, and then stiffened as her glance fell on the pillow next to her own. It bore the imprint of someone's head.

Shock trembled through her. Had those arms that held her not been merely a figment of her imagination, after all? Had Neil actually dared to take advantage of her drug-induced sleep and share this bed with her? For what purpose? she derided herself as she got unsteadily to her feet. Neil was hardly so likely to be starved of female company that he needed to make love to a half-comatose woman, especially a woman who had already shown herself to be more than willing to have him as her lover.

Had Neil slept there? She reached out and touched her fingers to the indented pillow, moving them gently over the shape of his head, tiny tremors of desire stirring her stomach. Dream or reality? She couldn't deny the fact that those arms wrapped round her body had brought her comfort and warmth, soothing away all her fears. She trembled a little more as she wondered what it would be like to spend all her nights wrapped in Neil's arms, and then told herself that she was being a fool to waste her time daydreaming about something that was never likely to happen.

She walked over to the window and stared outside. To judge from the height of the sun, it must be almost lunchtime. She had slept away almost an entire morning, something totally unheard of, and yet she couldn't deny that she felt rested and refreshed from her sleep.

From the window she could see as far as her own cottage, its rooftop just about visible over the high wall which separated it from the field, and her stomach began to churn nervously. How much damage had the fire done? Had it reached as far as the cottage? Had it destroyed the barn completely, and what about her drying shed?

Suddenly impatient to find out what was going on, she hurried into the bathroom, picking up the pile of clean clothes on her way. There was no one in sight as she went downstairs. She was dying for a cup of coffee, but the door to Neil's study stood open and she could hear men's voices coming from inside it.

Rue walked into the study and then came to an abrupt halt as she saw the three uniformed men talking with Neil. Two of them were policemen, and the other one, she guessed, must be the fire officer.

'Ah, here's Rue, now,' Neil told them, interrupting his conversation to turn towards her. He took hold of her arm and gently drew her into the room, pulling out a chair, and almost before she knew what she was doing Rue found that she was sitting down on it.

'Sorry to have to spring these questions on you while you're still suffering from the shock of last night,' one of the police officers said to Rue, 'but I'm afraid that there are certain questions that will have to be answered.'

Rue looked away from him and said urgently to Neil, 'The house, the barn...'

'Your home's quiet safe, Miss Livesey,' the fire officer told her calmly, answering her question for her. 'The barn, I'm afraid, has been virtually gutted, although we have managed to save the shell of it. The fire got as far as the drying shed and destroyed some of your stock, but the building itself is still standing.'

Rue felt so weak that she was glad that she was sitting down. She turned towards Neil, and noticed as she did so a huge pot of coffee on the desk in front of her. Her mouth started to water, and without asking her if she wanted some Neil pulled the tray towards him and poured her a mugful.

'We'll be taking criminal proceedings, of course,' one of the policemen announced, 'but in the meantime I expect you will want to claim against your insurance for the damage.'

'Criminal proceedings?' Rue stared at him in blank shock.

'Yes,' the man answered her, apparently unaware of her astonishment. 'It was very lucky for us that Mr Saxton cared enough about your situation to start making a few enquiries. Without the lead that he was able to give us, I doubt that we'd have been able to find the perpetrators quite as quickly.'

Rue looked from the policeman to Neil, her thoughts in turmoil.

'I'm sorry,' she said uncertainly. 'I'm afraid I don't understand. The fire was an accident, wasn't it?'

She made two discoveries simultaneously: one was that she was trembling from head to foot, the other was that Neil had somehow taken hold of her hand and that the heat radiating out from that point of contact was having a very disturbing effect on her already overstrained nervous system.

'Not exactly,' the police officer told her gravely. 'In fact, I'm afraid it looked very much as though the fire was started as a deliberate attempt to intimidate you. Mr Saxton has told us that this wasn't the first attempt to do so and that your dog was shot quite recently. Thanks to the information he was able to give us, we were able to act very quickly. We caught the two men who started the fire last night. Petty criminals who are relatively well-known to us, and they've admitted that they were paid to do the job by David Jenson.'

Rue stared at them. 'The builder? But why?' She looked helplessly at Neil. 'I don't understand any of this.'

'It's quite simple, really,' Neil told her soothingly. 'When Horatio had been shot, I made a few discreet enquiries of my own. No one from the village had been out shooting over my land, but someone did mention seeing a couple of strangers parking an old van well off the main road. He saw two men getting out of the van, one of them carrying a gun. What I couldn't work out at first was who would have a motive for shooting Horatio, and then you yourself answered that question without even knowing you were doing so.'

'How?' Rue asked him in bewilderment.

'You told me that the same builder who had wanted to buy your land and cottage had bought some farm land with no direct access to the main road, or to any road for that matter, and that the only way he could gain such access would be if he were somehow to gain possession of your land. Since I knew for myself how determined you were not to sell, when I discovered that Horatio had probably been deliberately shot I was immediately rather suspicious. Everyone knows how devoted you are to the dog, and it struck me that the builder may well have decided to institute a campaign of harassment against you, designed to get you to sell to him. The fire served two purposes at once,' he added grimly, 'both frightening you and destroying your business. That was one of the reasons I went to London,' he added obliquely. 'I have contacts up there who were able to find out much more about Jenson's way of doing business than I was able to do. When I learned that he didn't have a particularly good reputation for the way he achieved his business deals, my concern grew.'

'Why didn't you tell me about this?' Rue demanded shakily, completely forgetting their audience.

Neil looked at her, his steady grey gaze making her flush slightly. 'Would you have believed me?' he asked her quietly.

He had every right to make that quiet challenge. 'I don't know,' she admitted. 'It all sounds so very far-fetched.'

'Does it?' Neil asked her grimly. 'There was nothing imaginary about that fire last night.'

'If we could just ask you a few questions, Miss Livesey,' the police officer put in calmly, 'it won't take very long.'

It didn't, and Rue answered them as best she could, too shocked and astounded by the revelations Neil had made to be able to pay very much attention to the more mundane questions of the police officer.

An hour later, when the three of them had left, she turned to Neil and said shakily, 'I really ought to go back to the cottage. I must see how much damage has been done. You've been very kind, but . . .'

'I'll drive you there after we've had something to eat,' Neil told her tersely.

Now, when she needed his tenderness and compassion the most, to help her cope with the shock of what she had learned, he seemed to be distancing himself from her, deliberately holding himself aloof. It was very hard now, looking into his withdrawn features, to believe for one moment that this man had held her all through the night. That must have been a dream, she told herself tiredly, and the imprint on the other pillow probably her own.

'There's no need for you to go to so much trouble, Neil. You've already done more than enough.'

She started to shake suddenly as the full horror of what could have happened to her if he hadn't intervened suddenly struck her. She heard Neil curse as she suddenly swayed on her feet.

'What the hell are you trying to do to yourself?' he demanded gruffly. 'You don't have to prove anything to me, Rue,' he added with a savagery that dismayed her. 'I know how much you value your independence, how much you hate and abhor the idea of having to depend on anyone, especially on me,' he added angrily.

Rue had no idea what she had said or done to merit his anger, and as for her independence, she almost laughed aloud. She had lost that the day he had walked into her life.

CHAPTER TEN

In the event, it was three days before Rue's doctor pronounced her fit enough to be allowed to visit the cottage, and then only under Neil's supervision. She had apparently inhaled some smoke during her frantic attempts to rescue her stock, and this had resulted in a chest infection which made her lungs ache painfully and her body feel unfamiliarly weak.

So weak, in fact, that by the time she had walked round the house and seen for herself that it had not been touched by the fire she was more than glad of Neil's arm to lean on as he escorted her back to his car. Her head was thumping painfully, and she saw the now-familiar frown on his forehead as he had to match his steps to the slower pace of hers.

No wonder he was impatient with her; he must be sick and tired of the responsibility of her...a responsibility which he should by rights in no way have to shoulder. It was true that he was her closest neighbour, and it was equally true that both her doctor and the police seemed to think it only right and natural that she should be staying with him. She felt increasingly uncomfortable about it, though; she had no right to impinge on his privacy...or on his time.

Since that first night she had had no more dreams about him holding her, and she had come to the conclusion that that dream had been caused by her drug-induced sleep.

If Hannah had not been in Spain she would have got in touch with her and begged for her help, and it struck Rue, as she sat in a wicker chair in the conservatory wondering what on earth had happened to her old strength and energy, that although she had many, many acquaintances, there was no one she could actually turn to for the kind of succour Neil had given her.

He had so many calls upon his time that she could only marvel at and rather envy his dynamism. She had discovered while staying at the house that he kept in daily contact with his factory in Cambridge, via the very advanced computer installed in one of the cellars.

She had also learned inadvertently, through happening to walk past his open study door while he was on the telephone, that in addition to lecturing on the subject of advanced computer science he also gave generously and anonymously to several charities, mainly those that helped the socially and financially deprived.

Once a week a team of contract cleaners came to go through the house and leave it immaculate, but apart from that he had no other help, no housekeeper as her own father had had. He cooked his own meals and presumably dealt with his own laundry, although Rue doubted that he was actually personally responsible for his immaculately starched and ironed shirts.

She had never known a man who was so selfsufficient; her father, excellent scientist though he was, could barely make a cup of tea, and Julian... well, Julian, as she had discovered once she married him, expected to be waited on virtually hand and foot by the women in his life.

Neil, on the other hand, not only didn't need anyone to perform life's more mundane chores for him, he actually actively prevented her from doing so. He must want to make it plain to her that there was no role for her in his life. He had given no indication at all that he still desired her and, struggling to control her ever-growing love for him, Rue knew that she must either find a way of excluding him from her life completely, or accept that his proximity meant she would almost certainly spend the rest of her life suffering the torment of unrequited love.

She had spent most of the morning at the house with the insurance assessor, who had reassured her that she was adequately covered for the fire. He had further informed her that, under the terms of her insurance policy for the business, it was the insurance company's responsibility to provide someone to take charge of the day-to-day work with the flowers for the duration of her own incapacity.

Rue, who hadn't been able to remember such a clause in the policy, frowned now as she thought about it. There was no doubt that it was a relief to have everything taken care of, every burden lifted from her shoulders. The fire had affected her more than she had at first thought, both emotionally as well as physically.

The knowledge that someone could have set out to deliberately intimidate her without her even suspecting what was going on had left her feeling very vulnerable. Although she wouldn't for the world have admitted it to anyone, least of all Neil, she was growing increasingly reluctant to move back into the cottage. She was, for the first time since Julian's death, frightened of living on her own.

She moved restlessly in the cane chair. Neil was in Cambridge on business and, as always when he was away, she missed him. Not that he spent much time with her, seeming actually to avoid her company whenever he could.

Perhaps the best thing she could do would be to sell the cottage and its land to Neil and make a fresh start somewhere else. Somewhere where she wouldn't be constantly tormented by his presence. As Neil himself pointed out to her, with the money from the sale she could buy herself a small property and live quite comfortably on her investment. It would have to be in the country, of course. Horatio would never adopt to city living. She might even find a job.

Neil walked in while she was mulling over the wisest thing to do.

The sight of him, as always, had a very definite physical effect on her body, its reaction to him so immediate and strong that she still hadn't found a way to control it. Instead she turned away from him, pretending to be absorbed in the view from the conservatory window. When her father had owned the Court, she had rarely used this room, but now she found it a relaxing and secure haven.

When she had herself sufficiently under control, she turned and looked warily at Neil. He looked drained and tired, tiny lines of exhaustion fanning out around his eyes.

'Wouldn't it make life much easier for you if you lived closer to the factory?' she asked him impulsively, concerned for the strain he constantly put himself under.

Immediately he frowned angrily, and demanded, 'Still trying to get rid of me, Rue? I'm sorry, but

I'm not about to oblige you. I've had to work damned hard all my life. My father died when I was seven and I watched my mother struggle to find the money for us to live. I swore then that things were going to be different, and now that they are I sure as hell am not going to spend my precious free time cooped up in a high-rise apartment!

'There comes a time in a man's life...and a woman's...when you have to decide what you want from life...what it is you're striving for. More success...more money...more pressure to attain more and more power...or something else? My business is successful. I can make as much money as I need without pushing myself any harder.

'Twelve months ago I came to a decision. I looked around myself and at my own life, and what I saw made me stop and take stock. I'm thirty-five years old. I've got a successful business and I'm a wealthy man. During the years I was building the business I deliberately avoided getting myself involved in any kind of committed relationship. There wasn't time, it was too much of a risk...you name it, I used every excuse there was to keep myself from admitting the truth.' He swung round and looked hard at her. 'Shall I tell you what that truth is, Rue? Shall I tell you what I've had to learn about myself? You'd do well to listen, because there's something you could learn from my mistakes...'

He had never spoken to her like this before...never told her so much about his own background, his thoughts and feelings. Her mouth felt dry, and she touched her tongue-tip to her lips nervously, not sure if she was going to like what she was about to hear.

'I looked around and saw that the majority of my peers had wives and families... they had homes and hobbies... they went on holidays... In short, they had and did all the things I had deliberately excluded from my life. I looked at them, and I looked at myself, and for the first time in my life I asked myself if the price I had decided to pay for my success had been worth while, and I made myself face up to the fact that it wasn't because I was building up the business that I had refused to get involved in any kind of emotional commitment, it was because I was running scared. Scared not of commitment, but of loss... of loving someone and losing them, the way my mother had lost my father...'

Rue hesitated for a long time after listening to his impassioned speech, and then she asked him uncertainly, 'And that's why you bought this house?'

'I bought this house as an act of faith... as a commitment to myself, if you like, that my life was going to change, that it was going to contain all the things it had previously lacked. Be careful *you* don't make the same mistakes I made, Rue,' he told her abruptly. 'Be careful *you* don't wake up at night and find out what it really means to be completely alone.'

She swallowed painfully, wondering what he would say if she told him she had already discovered that she knew the pain that came from such loneliness.

Instead she said brightly, 'I suppose that, now you've got a house, the next thing you'll be looking for will be a wife.'

Her heart started thumping as he gave her a cool look and then said quietly, 'You suppose quite right.'

'I don't imagine you'll have to look far,' she told him, determined not to let him see the effect his announcement was having on her. 'I'm sure there must be any number of women only too willing to marry you.'

She tried to make her voice sound mocking and faintly derisory, desperate to conceal her inner pain.

'Unlike you... You're not the marrying kind, are you, Rue?' he said grimly. 'You prefer your independence.'

He couldn't have made it plainer that she was the last woman he would consider as a wife. She swallowed painfully and whispered, 'Yes, that's right. Marriage isn't something I want. After all, I'm not like you, Neil; I've tried it once.' She got up unsteadily. 'If you don't mind, I think I'll go upstairs for a rest.'

She saw him frown. 'Are your lungs still bothering you? The doctor...'

'I'm tired, that's all,' she interrupted him bleakly, and then added bitterly, 'You seem to forget that this isn't my home, Neil. I'm not used to sharing my living space with someone else.'

He stood up too, giving her an angry look, his mouth set in a bitter line.

'You don't need to go on. I get the message,' he told her grimly.

In her room, Rue didn't rest as she had told Neil she was going to do, but instead reached for the telephone he had considerately had installed for her, and dialled the number of her solicitor.

He seemed surprised when she gave him her instructions, and no wonder, Rue reflected wryly as she hung up. After all, it wasn't so very long ago that she had sworn that she would never, never sell her home, and yet here she was changing her mind, telling him to write to Neil's solicitors and inform them that if Neil still wanted to buy the house and land she was prepared to sell them to him.

Knowing the laboriously slow way in which legal wheels turned, Rue guessed it would be several days before Neil learned of her change of heart, by which time she would have removed herself from his proximity permanently.

Now that the decision was made she would need to organise herself. She would need somewhere temporary to live...

Luckily it was almost the end of the summer. She ought to be able to rent a holiday cottage without too much difficulty. The local estate agent could probably help her with that, and once she was safely away from Neil she could start to make proper plans for what she was going to do with her future. A bleak and empty future without him, but, listening to his plans for his own life, it had become depressingly clear to her that there was no way she could remain living in the village watching him with his wife and family, slowly growing more and more embittered and alone.

There would be time enough tomorrow to start making formal plans. Now she felt as drained and in need of a rest as she had claimed. Her muscles ached with tension and she glanced towards the closed bathroom door. A warm bath to relax her, and then a brief sleep. She grimaced wryly to herself as she headed for the door. That was all she seemed to do these days, eat and sleep, and yet, strangely, she had not gained any weight...did not feel any real benefit from her relaxation. And, if anything, the tension inside her seemed to grow and go on growing.

She was immersed in the warm, soapy water when the communicating door to the other bedroom opened abruptly and Neil strode in.

He was half-way across the room, heading for the opposite door, when he stopped abruptly, realising she was in the bath.

Rue had never felt more self-conscious or more embarrassed in all her life.

As he stared at her she made instinctive and totally ineffective efforts to conceal her nudity, at the same time demanding breathlessly, 'Go away!'

'Not yet. Not until you've told me exactly what you're playing at,' Neil told her grimly.

'Playing at?' Rue stared at him in confusion. 'I'm having a bath.'

His glance flickered from her face down to where the wet curves of her breasts rose above the foamy water. Her flesh tingled as she saw the sudden hard burn of colour darken his cheekbones.

And then he had himself under control and was looking back into her eyes, his own dark with anger.

'That isn't what I meant and you know it,' he told her tersely. 'My solicitor's just been on the phone.'

Now it was Rue's skin that burned, in a hot, betraying tide of colour that seemed to start at her toes and sweep all the way up her body, until there was no part of her that hadn't pinkened under her guilty flush.

She had counted on Neil's not finding out about her decision until she was too far away from him to question her, because if there was one thing she had learned about him it was that he was not the kind of man to take anything at face value, and she knew that he would question and delve into the reason for her abrupt change of mind until she was in danger of revealing the truth to him.

And that was the last thing she wanted to do.

He looked at her for so long that the pink flush darkened to bright scarlet and, although she longed passionately for him to go away, it was no longer because her nudity embarrassed her, but because she was afraid of what he might make her say.

'Why the change of heart, Rue?' he asked her quietly.

If only she had had the forethought to prepare herself for this interview. If only she had not rushed foolishly into action. If only she had waited until she had already left before getting in touch with her solicitor...

She fought to maintain some degree of self-possession and said huskily, 'I know this is your home, Neil, but surely I'm entitled to some privacy? Can't we discuss this later, when I'm dressed? The water's getting cold,' she added, giving a genuine shudder.

'You'd better get out of the bath, then, hadn't you?' he told her unemotionally, adding, 'I'm not a complete fool, Rue. If I give you the opportunity, you'll disappear without telling me what the hell's going on.'

Rue stared at him in disbelief. He didn't expect her to get out of the bath with him standing there, did he? It seemed that he did, and when he saw her hesitation he looked at her grimly and said, 'Don't move.'

When he opened the door and walked into the other bedroom she was half tempted to get out of the bath and make a dash for her own room, but she was glad she had resisted the urge when he returned in less than two minutes carrying a thick towelling robe.

'Here, put this on,' he told her, handing it to her and then turning his back.

The water had gone cold and she shivered as she stepped out of it, her fingers clumsy as she pushed her arms into the robe, which was many sizes too big for her. The faint, elusive musk that clung to it was Neil's, she recognised, her body reacting to the intimate scent of another human being.

'This is *your* robe,' she said almost accusingly as he turned to face her. 'What was it doing in that room? Your bedroom is right down the end of the landing.'

'Is it? What makes you think that?' Neil asked her.

Uncertainly Rue looked at the half-open door.

'I moved into this bedroom because Hannah said the decorators would probably want to start on the master suite first, and just as well I did, too. The first night you were here you had a nightmare, and you were screaming fit to raise the dead.'

Rue's mouth went dry, her whole body suddenly tense, the question she had to ask trembling on her lips. She stared at him, her eyes enormous with despair and pain.

'I tried to wake you up,' Neil continued drily, 'but you were too deeply under—not so deeply, though, that you were going to let me go.'

'Let you go?' Rue demanded chokily, her chest tight with anxiety. 'What do you mean?'

'Only that when I leaned over you to try to wake you up you put your arms around me and whispered that you wanted me to stay.'

'No,' Rue protested, but even as she made the denial she wasn't sure of her ground. She had no recollection of that night at all, apart from those fragmented memories of a bad dream about the fire, followed by the blissful comfort of being held and comforted...

'Yes!' Neil insisted. 'Yes! You opened your eyes and looked at me and told me that you wanted me to stay. You spent the whole night sleeping in my arms.'

'I didn't know what I was doing,' she told him huskily. Suddenly it had become imperative that she convince him that her behaviour had meant nothing. 'Anyway,' she added wildly, 'that isn't important now. If you don't want to buy my property, Neil, then all you have to do is to say so. No doubt I can find another buyer.'

'No doubt,' he agreed, and then demanded, 'Why the rush to sell, Rue?'

'I don't feel the same about the cottage now. After the fire...' She gave a shudder that wasn't entirely faked.

'Are you sure it *is* just the fear of your memories of the fire you're running away from?' he asked her softly.

Something in the way he was looking at her alerted her to her danger. 'Of course,' she responded defensively. 'What else could it be?'

'This,' he told her succinctly, closing the space between them and taking hold of her, sliding his hands up under the cuffs of the too-large robe, his fingertips stroking her skin and raising rashes of goose-bumps along her arms.

Her entire body trembled beneath his touch, her eyes wide and dark, betraying her fear.

'I think you're running away because you're frightened of the way I make you feel. You're running away because you can't face up to the fact that you want me...'

'No,' Rue denied desperately, as his head bent closer, his breath scorching her skin.

'No, what?' he murmured between light kisses against her forehead. 'No, you're not frightened, or no, you don't want me? If it's the latter, you're lying, Rue, and I can prove it to you...'

Before she could stop him, his hand moved from her arm and parted the front of her borrowed robe, reaching out to cup the soft weight of her breast.

A shiver of delicious sensation quivered through her, a sharp cry of tension bubbling in her throat as his thumb stroked slowly back and forth over her nipple, wordlessly telling her that he knew quite well the effect he had on her.

All at once the fight went out of her, and instead of resisting him as she knew she ought to she said wildly, 'Yes, it's true. I *do* want you, and I *am* frightened of that wanting. Can't you understand, Neil? The only other man who's made love to me hurt me badly. Isn't it understandable that I should be scared?'

She saw the look in his eyes and realised with a fierce leap of her heart that he liked knowing there'd been no one else apart from Julian. Her mouth went dry, her body shaking so much that she was sure that if he hadn't been holding her she would have collapsed.

'There's nothing to be frightened of, Rue,' he told her thickly. 'I won't hurt you.'

But she knew he would...because he didn't know the *truth*...didn't know that she *loved* him. She had managed to keep that much from him, if nothing else.

'It's no good, Neil,' she cried out feverishly. 'We can't be lovers...'

'We already are,' he told her, shocking her immobile until he laughed softly and added, 'Oh, not literally, perhaps—I didn't take advantage of you during your drugged sleep, if that's what you're thinking—but you know and I know that we *are* lovers, Rue. There's never been a woman who's made me feel the way you do, and I suspect that no other man has aroused you as I can.'

It was all too painfully true, but she had to stop him somehow, to make him realise...and then abruptly she knew there was only one way, only one weapon she could use now to deflect him from his purpose.

Steadily she looked at him.

'I want you physically, Neil...I can't deny it. But can't you see: your physical possession of me would never be enough? I'd want more. Much more than you're prepared to give,' she admitted painfully. 'I'd want your love as well as your lovemaking, Neil. I'd want more from you than just a brief affair.'

She waited for him to release her, to turn away from her with shocked embarrassment, to tell her that she was right and that he had been wrong, but to her astonishment he just continued to look at her and then said hoarsely, 'Say that again!'

His face had lost all its colour, his bones standing out tautly. He swallowed, and she saw the movement in the rigid muscles of his throat. His hand tightened on her arm, the fingers caressing her breast suddenly stilling.

She had come too far to lose her courage now. One quick blow...an instant severing now was surely less painful in the long run than gradually waiting for him to discover the truth and then reject her.

'I'm in love with you, Neil,' she told him sadly. 'That's why I want to sell the cottage...to move away...'

To her astonishment, instead of releasing her, he said roughly, 'I don't believe it! You're even more of a coward than I thought. I could find it in my heart to forgive you when I thought you just weren't aware of your feelings, but to stand here and listen to you telling me that you'd rather turn your back on what we feel for one another than give up your independence... At least you haven't suggested we become part-time lovers, you in your cottage, me here...because that *is* something I could never stomach. Perhaps you're right—I'd want all of you or nothing at all. Commitment, marriage, a family and everything that that means...and you're not prepared to make that commitment, are you, Rue? You're not prepared to give up your freedom and independence. They mean more to you than I do.'

He was white to his lips, every word he spoke almost spat out at her as he fought with his rage. Rue knew she ought to be terrified, but all she could do was simply stand and stare at him in disbelief.

She reached out her hand and touched him shakily, interrupting his tirade.

'Neil...I don't understand. When you spoke about marriage, about love, I thought you were warning me that there would inevitably be someone else...that all you could ever feel for me would be a fleeting desire. In fact, I thought you didn't even want me any more.'

'Not want you?' He stared at her, his tension dying, to be replaced by a look of grim self-mockery. 'For a woman of your years, you know remarkably little about men, my dear. Ever since I walked into this room, my body has been proclaiming extremely obviously and painfully exactly what effect you have on me.'

Round-eyed, Rue's glance slid down his body, coming to rest on his thighs, her skin pinkening betrayingly at his unmistakable arousal.

'Why the hell did you pretend that you didn't care?' Neil groaned rawly. 'I've been going out of my mind trying to think of ways to keep you here so that I could convince you that what we could have between us was worth far more than independence, but every time I brought the subject up, every response you made only seemed to confirm how determined you were not to allow any commitment between us. You don't *know* how desperately close I've come to giving in to my baser needs and making love to you regardless.'

'Why didn't you?' Rue asked him shakily.

'Because, like you, I wanted more than sexual satisfaction,' he told her frankly. 'I knew I could make you desire me, but that wasn't enough, and I was terrified that once we'd been lovers you'd refuse to even contemplate accepting me emotionally.

'Much as I wanted you physically, to enter into a relationship with you based merely on physical desire would have demeaned all that I felt for you. I've never believed in love at first sight—nor love at all, really—but when you opened your cottage door to me and stood there looking at me so aggressively, I felt as though the sky had fallen in on me.'

'You knew *then*?' Rue asked him disbelievingly.

'I knew then,' he confirmed. 'I've waited a long time to meet the woman I want to spend the rest of my life with. It nearly tore me apart to know that I'd found her and that she didn't share my feelings.'

'I did, though,' Rue admitted, 'but I was so scared of them . . . so terrified.'

'That I'd hurt you as Julian did,' Neil supplied drily, but Rue shook her head.

'No, I never feared that, not really. I'm not a complete fool, Neil. Julian had an unusually self-destructive personality, and I was too selfish and spoilt to see it when I met him. No, I knew you'd never hurt me, at least not deliberately, but I was frightened of the way I feel about you . . . frightened of getting into a situation which could only cause me pain. You see, I thought all you wanted was an affair. I thought you kept going on about my independence because you wanted to make it plain to me that you didn't want me permanently in your life.'

She heard him groan and then laugh. 'When I think of the time we've wasted,' he muttered huskily against her hair.

Somehow or other, both his hands had slid inside the robe and were caressing her body. Free of her fears, she was able to respond to him the way she ached to be able to. She felt him shudder as she pressed herself eagerly against him, moaning softly in her throat as his hands cupped her breasts, tantalising their hard, erect peaks.

She reached up to him and put her arms round his neck, urging his head down towards her own, her lips parting provocatively.

He touched them with his tongue, as though testing their texture and taste, and then stroked them moistly before sliding his tongue-tip between her teeth.

Rue moaned again against the deliberate thrust of his tongue, pressing deeper into him, shivering with pleasure when he parted the robe and pushed his thigh between hers.

She could feel the hard, hot pressure of his erection against her stomach. Her fingers clutched at his arms, her head bending back under the pressure of his kiss, her hips moving frantically against him in open invitation.

'Somehow I always knew you'd be like this,' he told her against her mouth. 'Warm, eager...loving.' Her hips rotated yearningly against him and he groaned, his body shuddering.

'Have you any idea what you're doing to me?' he protested, and against his mouth Rue said huskily,

'No, but if it's anything at all like what you're doing to me, I think...'

She gasped out loud as his hand swept down the side of her body and across the taut muscles of her belly, unerringly finding the place where she ached and pulsed so tormentingly, and as though he knew immediately how great her need was he picked her up and carried her, not into her own room, but into his, depositing her gently on the large bed.

'I think this is not so much the first time we're making love as the culmination of the way we should have made love that morning in your kitchen,' he muttered as he stripped off his clothes and came to her.

His body was all muscle and taut, supple skin warm like heavy satin, so pleasurable to touch that she felt almost drunk on the sensation of doing so, and for a while he let her, simply holding her while she gathered in through her fingertips a vast wealth of intense pleasure; and all the time, beyond *that* pleasure, lay another, deeper, sharper, waiting to be released... building like the tightening of a coiled wire to a pitch where she was almost quivering with the intensity of it, every part of her body so alive that she was practically vibrating with sharp anticipation.

At last he said quietly, 'No more, Rue,' and he took her hands away from his body and turned to her so that she could see what she had made him.

She was poised and waiting for him, her body moist and eager to receive him, anticipation strung so tightly inside her that his first slow thrust made her cry out her pleasure to him, wrapping herself around him and drawing him deeper and deeper inside her until her whole body pulsed in the same fierce rhythm that drove him.

Beneath her hands his back was slick with sweat, the scent of him enveloping her, the fierce drum of his heart pounding against her.

Even though she had never experienced it before, her body seemed to know instinctively how to invite his to drive ever deeper within it so that the pleasure built up into an almost unbearable tension, its sudden climactic release almost more than she could endure.

She felt the spasms of release shudder through Neil and clung to him, welcoming the heat of him within her own flesh, relaxing into his arms as he held her and stroked her damp skin, easing her down beside him, her head resting in the curve of his shoulder.

'I'd forgotten that you're still supposed to be recuperating,' he apologised to her, but Rue only laughed.

'I certainly need to now,' she told him teasingly, watching the dark colour run up under his skin with possessive amusement.

'It's been one hell of a long time,' he muttered, avoiding looking at her. 'I gave up going in for casual affairs years ago, and the kind of life I've been living doesn't allow for anything else.'

His confession surprised and pleased her.

'How long is a long time?' she asked him curiously.

'A couple of years at least,' he admitted. 'That's why I've been finding it so damned hard to keep my hands off you. You're committed to me now, Rue,' he told her rawly. 'And don't even think of changing your mind, because I'm not about to let you go. You realise that you could already be carrying my child?' he added starkly.

Rue had, but only in the last few seconds. Oddly, she found the thought tantalisingly pleasurable.

'In that case, I suppose I'll have to make an honest man of you,' she teased him, letting him see the love in her eyes, adding with a small secret smile, 'Of course, I might not be pregnant...'

'Do you *want* my child?' Neil demanded hoarsely, correctly reading the message in her eyes. His were glittering almost feverishly as he waited for her answer, and she realised, as she had not before, how much the thought of a wife and family really meant to him.

'Yes,' she told him honestly, suddenly feeling very shaky and emotional. 'Yes, I do.' She reached out and traced his mouth with her fingertip. 'I want *our* children very much indeed, Neil.'

'But your work...your independence...'

'I worked because I felt I had to prove to myself that I wasn't still the same selfish, heedless child Julian had married. I never had any desire to become a successful business-woman. I just wanted to prove that I was a person in my own right...and now I *have* proved it! There'll be plenty to keep me occupied here running this house, helping you. I don't know much about computers yet, but I can always learn.'

She felt him tense and wondered what she had said, looking at him uncertainly and asking hesitantly, 'What's wrong?'

'I want you again,' he told her thickly. 'Oh, Rue, what is it that you do to me?'

'I don't know,' she told him mock-seriously, 'but you have exactly the same effect on me.' She turned to him and moved her body against him. 'Make love to me again, Neil, and prove to me that I'm not dreaming all this.'

'If you are, we're dreaming it together,' he muttered against her mouth. 'I love you, Rue, and I'm never going to stop proving it to you—never.'

'I believe you,' she told him, and it was true!

HARLEQUIN
American Romance®

THE ROMANCE THAT STARTED IT ALL!

For Diane Bauer and Nick Granatelli, the walk down the aisle was a rocky road....

Don't miss the romantic prequel to WITH THIS RING—

I THEE WED
BY ANNE McALLISTER

Harlequin American Romance #387

Let Anne McAllister take you to Cambridge, Massachusetts, to the night when an innocent blind date brought a reluctant Diane Bauer and Nick Granatelli together. For Diane, a smoldering attraction like theirs had only one fate, one future—marriage. The hard part, she learned, was convincing her intended....

Watch for Anne McAllister's I THEE WED, available *now* from Harlequin American Romance.

ITW

**If you loved American Romance #387
I THEE WED...**

You are cordially invited to attend the
wedding of Diane Bauer and
Nick Granatelli....

**ONE WEDDING—FOUR LOVE STORIES
FROM YOUR FAVORITE HARLEQUIN
AUTHORS!**

**BETHANY CAMPBELL
BARBARA DELINSKY
BOBBY HUTCHINSON
ANN McALLISTER**

*The church is booked, the reception arranged and the
invitations mailed. All Diane and Nick have to do is walk
down the aisle. Little do they realize that the most cherished
day of their lives will spark so many romantic notions....*

Available wherever Harlequin books are sold.

You'll flip . . . your pages won't!
Read paperbacks *hands-free* with

Book Mate · I

The perfect "mate" for all your romance paperbacks

Traveling • Vacationing • At Work • In Bed • Studying • Cooking • Eating

Perfect size for all standard paperbacks, this wonderful invention makes reading a pure pleasure! Ingenious design holds paperback books OPEN and FLAT so even wind can't ruffle pages – leaves your hands free to do other things. Reinforced, wipe-clean vinyl-covered holder flexes to let you turn pages without undoing the strap . . . supports paperbacks so well, they have the strength of hardcovers!

Pages turn WITHOUT opening the strap

SEE-THROUGH STRAP

Reinforced back stays flat

Built in bookmark

BOOK MARK

BACK COVER HOLDING STRIP

10 x 7¼ opened
Snaps closed for easy carrying, too